MAR 2 3 2022

PRAISE FOR LAURA KEMP

Action and suspense combine with magic and compassion to create and exciting and satisfying ending for a twisting tale. Thank you for the adventure and the tears, Mrs. Kemp.

— NOLA NASH ~ AWARD WINNING AUTHOR OF
THE CRESCENT CITY SERIES

A stunning conclusion to a brilliant trilogy. Laura Kemp's skill shines on every page of "A Home for the Stars" as she deftly navigates complex characters through emotional quandaries, supernatural folklore, and edge of your seat action. Take a breath and hope the story continues.

— ROB SAMBORN ~ AUTHOR OF PRISONER OF
PARADISE

As a Michigan boy, I was drawn to Lantern Creek because it felt like home. "A Home for the Stars" ties the series up with a bow, with equal parts, sci-fy, mystery and romance. It's a tale you will want to return to again and again.

— TERRY SHEPHERD ~ AUTHOR OF THE JESSICA
RAMIREZ THRILLERS

D1260395

A HOME FOR THE STARS

LAURA KEMP

Ramirez & Clark
PUBLISHERS

Copyright © 2022 by Laura Kemp

All rights reserved.

ISBN:

Paperback: 978-1-955171-16-8

Hardcover: 978-1-955171-17-5

No part of this book may be reproduced in any form or by any electronic or mechanical means, including information storage and retrieval systems, without written permission from the author, except for the use of brief quotations in a book review.

This is a work of fiction. Unless otherwise indicated, all the names, characters, businesses, places, events and incidents in this book are either the product of the author's imagination or used in a fictitious manner. Any resemblance to actual persons, living or dead, or actual events is purely coincidental.

To my kids... the beat goes on.

PROLOGUE

'I just keep on making the same mistakes, hoping that you'll understand.' -*Ed Sheeran*

I was falling, the cold numbing my bones in a way that made me feel like I'd been caught in a storm blowing in from the Big Lake. I reached out, expecting to touch the soft sheets on the bed I shared with Dylan and felt something scratch my fingertips.

I pulled my hand back quickly.

"Dad?" I whispered, wondering if he would come to me.

Silence punctured by the sharp needle of a male voice.

ADAM? WHERE ARE YOU?

My mind fluttered to the image of my brother crumbling beneath the butt of Henry Younts' shotgun. I felt the heavy press of despair, the darkness holding me tight when I needed space.

I thought of Dylan, wanting to feel the curl of his body against

1

me, wondering where he was and why he'd left me alone in this strange place when a soft voice joined the first.

"She'll be all right, Ma."

And a third voice- higher, and with a hint of annoyance.

"Will she, then? And who will feed her, I'd like to know?"

I shifted on what I thought might be a bed, felt a sharp pain in my side and remembered the moment the buckshot had sprayed across my hip like droplets of scalding water.

The sounds rose again, the male voice closer as a hand slid across the bare flesh of my stomach. I started, reached down to stop their progress but something told me to wait, that the hands were there to help.

I tried to open my eyes but found myself standing on the snowy moss instead.

Troy was there, watching me as he had under the deck lights at the Pink Pony.

"Where am I?" I asked, my voice hollow in my ears.

"We're trying to find you," he answered. And I knew he was telling the truth, knew that he would never stop trying.

"Where's Adam?"

"He's okay," he said. "We're taking care of him."

I looked to my feet, to the place where my brother had fallen, and saw nothing.

"Dylan," his name caught in my throat.

"He's gone after you."

"Gone after me?" I asked, hearing the strange voices again- the hands moving just above my hip. "Where am I?"

"Don't you remember?" he asked, and I looked into his eyes, the same eyes I felt could see through me and remembered our time in the clearing on Mackinac Island. The air had been heavy, the breeze languid as it caressed my body.

I remembered driving in Dylan's truck to a place where the snow fell in summer, remembered standing on the Whisper Stone as a great wind carried me away.

But where had it taken me?

"Is Amanda here?" I asked, thinking of the girl who had jumped from Robinson's Folly and the bridge that connected the world I recognized to this strange, in-between place.

"There's no path for her," he said.

I thought about what he'd said and felt like I would understand in time.

"Am I lost?" I asked.

He nodded. "You need to find the medicine bag."

Yes... I remembered that, remembered that I needed to stop Henry Younts before he hurt the people I loved. And this was the only way... even Dylan had agreed when he tricked Sara Bennett into getting us here.

I watched Troy take a step backwards and felt fear cinch my chest.

"Don't go," I said, one hand rising to touch him.

"Find what you came here for," he said. "It's the only way to save us."

He moved again, closer to the darkness and I tensed, felt the blanket slide sideways against my skin.

"Troy," I said his name, heard the word echo against the darkness that brushed my vision and felt the dream peel away.

The room was dim and tinted with the mellow light of a kerosene lamp. I was alone apart from a young woman who stood in a far corner, watching. I tried to focus and saw that she was small, like me, her blond hair plaited in a long braid that hung over her shoulder.

I blinked, trying to place her- feeling like I should be able to.

"You're awake," she said, coming to me quickly, her hands clasped at her waist. "I'm so glad."

I drew a breath, my mind wandering to the voices and the deck lights, and the way Troy had looked at me.

"Doc gave you a tonic to make you sleep. We were afraid he might have given you too much."

"Doc?" I repeated, feeling dumb, remembering the hands on my stomach again.

"He came as soon as we called- right after Cal found you in the field."

Yes, I remembered stumbling up to a small house on the edge of the woods beside a boy who looked like my brother. I remembered clutching my bloody side while scanning for any sign of Dylan or Amanda.

"Lucky that buckshot didn't kill you."

I nodded, not wanting to betray my terror, and as she sank into the chair beside my bed, I couldn't help but stare.

She was slim, her simple cotton dress accentuating the curves of a woman who looked to be in her late twenties. Her eyes were dark, a contrast to her honey blond hair, her lips pursed in consternation.

"I wanted to call for the shaman," she said, her words sending a jolt through me. "But Ma wouldn't allow it."

"Butler?" I asked, the sound of his name startling her as she stiffened on her chair.

"You know of him?"

I didn't know how to answer, and so I tried to sit up only to discover that I was naked beneath the blanket. I crossed my arms against my chest, trying to shield myself from her gaze but she didn't seem to notice.

"Johnny burned your clothes."

I felt a wave of panic capsize me as I reached for my throat, relief sweeping my skin when I felt the necklace.

"He what?" I asked.

"He burned them," she repeated. "I have a dress you can wear. Ma can make you another."

"Thank you..." I stammered. "But why did you say you wanted the shaman to help me?"

The woman smiled; a lovely thing that made me feel like a child who had just felt sunshine on her face. "He would have given

4

you something better. Something that wouldn't make you scream."

I sank down beneath the blanket, my fingers going to my stomach, feeling a strange cloth around my waist.

"Did Doc do this?" I asked, remembering the moment I had wanted to stop the hands.

"Yes," the woman answered.

"And I screamed?"

"Yes," She nodded again, her dark eyes large as she leaned forward. "You were saying their names over and over."

"Who?" I asked, a memory materializing from the jumble of my mind.

"Adam and Dylan," she said. "Are they your people?"

"My people?" I repeated, unable to understand. "I love them."

"They are, then," she smiled again. "We'll help you find them."

I felt a warmth spread to my chest, the voices on the other side of the door rising until a knock sounded, high and fast. I started, clutching the blanket as the door swung open on its hinges and a stout woman who could have seemed cheerful under different circumstances entered the room.

"You need to tend to the boy's supper," she said, her tone brusque as she wiped a sheen of sweat from her upper lip with the back of her hand. "I'll take care of her."

The young woman stood, her skirts rustling on the plank floor.

"Wait," I said, not knowing why. "What's your name?"

She smiled again, turned to walk out the door and in that moment, I remembered everything.

"Odessa."

CHAPTER
ONE

Calvert Cook stood and listened to the strange girl crying out behind the door of the bedroom his ma and gran shared. His Uncle Johnny was standing beside him, his wide face bunched up in a way that made him look like he'd been sucking on lemons. He held his floppy hat between his hands, twisting it tightly when she yelled again.

"Where'd she come from?" he asked, and Cal frowned. His uncle had asked that question twice before and Cal had answered each time.

But that was the trouble with Johnny, he sometimes forgot things.

"I was bringing Lolly into the barn and there she was, just lying in the field with blood on her blouse."

Now she was calling for someone named Dylan and Cal wondered if he was her beau and what he would think of them burning up all her clothes.

As if on cue, Johnny turned and looked down on his nephew.

"You don't think that feller o' hers will be mad at me for setting fire to her garments?" he looked away, his clear eyes worried. "They was the strangest things I ever seen."

Cal agreed. In all his twelve years on earth he'd never seen so much of a woman's body, and the thought made him feel like he'd been caught peeking at Ana Cuppy as she played on the schoolyard swings.

"It was like she was wearin' her unmentionables," Johnny explained, his cheeks red. "Only they was on the *outside!*"

Another shout. Another name. And this time his ma came out through the door, her face flushed.

"You need to fetch some fresh bandages and iodine," she said quickly. "We need to change her dressing."

"Did Doc get the buckshot out?" he asked, wondering if she was all right, feeling like he might be sorry if she wasn't.

"Mostly," she whispered, looking at her brother who stood in place, his hands twisting the hat. She took Cal's shoulder and pulled him away, her voice lowered. "Fetch the cherry bark tea Butler made for you when he took you to the woods."

Cal's shoulders stiffened, and not because he didn't want to obey, but because of his Uncle Johnny and Gran.

They didn't like the shaman and disapproved of him spending time with Cal, telling the boy more than once that he was filling his head with wickedness.

But he wasn't worried about what his gran and uncle thought because ever since Butler had come looking for work, Cal had stuck close to his side.

His ma hadn't gone far, either, and Cal suspected the shaman was sweet on her. He would never admit it to his uncle or gran or anyone for that matter because ever since they'd started attending River Run Church, the preacher made it clear he wanted to court his mother.

Not that Cal was happy about that.

He didn't like the preacher... didn't trust him, even though they had been faithful churchgoers for almost a year now.

8

Most Sundays he took off for the woods after they made their way home, him and his ma and uncle walking the dusty road and Gran atop their old mare, Lolly. He always told his ma that he was going to read his Bible in back of the shed, when really he would sneak off to the little cabin over the next rise that Butler had decided to keep as his own.

It seemed the shaman expected him now as he seemed to always be waiting, rising from his chair by the fire to walk in the woods. It was there, deep in the quiet reaches of the forest that he would tell him about different plants and how they could help the people he loved.

He'd told him once not long ago that there was a better way to help them, something beyond what even the earth could provide. When Cal asked, he told him it was something that had been taught to him by his father and grandfather beside the fires of his clan and Cal wanted to know so badly it made his heart ache.

But Butler told him it was not time yet, that all the things needed had not been found and it would do no good to begin without them and-

"Calvert Cook!" his ma yelled, and he started. She never did that.

"Yes?" he asked, his eyes large and at once his ma's face softened as she knelt in front of him.

"I told you to run to the shed and fetch the cherry bark tea. Doc got most of the buckshot out but if she keeps moving it'll get infected, and then she'll be in a world of hurt."

"Infected," he repeated, feeling that strange tug again that said he would be sad if something happened to her.

"She's in a lot of pain and your gran won't give her more laudanum if it means she has to go without."

Cal nodded. He'd already known his gran was nursing her bottle, waiting for the next time Doc agreed to give her more.

"Don't worry about what they say if they see you," his ma said,

her smile reminding him of why Butler hadn't moved on. "I'll take care of it."

Cal nodded again.

"Go."

He turned quickly, opened the door to the darkness and hurried up the path towards the shed where his uncle kept the tack for Lolly. Once there, he opened the door slowly, careful not to be seen or heard.

Butler had shown him the bark of the cherry tree during one of their first walks together. He had taken out a beautiful knife with a bone handle and cut some of the young branches off, then they had gone together to his cabin where they boiled them gently in a pot heated over the fire. The liquid had cooled, and Cal watched as Butler poured it into a glass jar, telling him to hide it in the shed because it was a gift for his ma.

Cal smiled, his brown eyes settling on the man who wanted to help them, and Butler had smiled in return- a brilliant thing that made Cal feel like everything was going to be all right.

He grabbed the same glass jar now, hidden away in a secret corner under a blanket and started back towards the house when another figure stepped into view- a large man he knew even in the darkness.

"Calvert," he said, his tone heavy with a kind of importance he had given himself.

"P-Preacher Younts," he answered, his heart skittering away like the deer he saw at dusk.

He heard the preacher clear his throat, saw one hand reach up to stroke the whiskers that darkened his chin. "I hear there's a girl at your place who needs prayin' over."

Cal shifted from foot to foot, his hands clasping the jar.

"Is that true?" Preacher barked, and Cal shrank down. "I can see your ma needs a man in the house to take you in hand."

"W-we got Uncle Johnny," Cal stammered, a thing he seemed to do whenever Henry Younts spoke to him.

The large man laughed, his hand clamping down on Cal's shoulder. "I'd call Johnson Cook a thing or two, but man ain't one of them."

Cal looked towards the house, thinking of Butler and his wide smile, wanting to feel like everything was all right again.

"Does that girl need prayin' over or not?"

Cal nodded; the jar slippery in his hands. "She was hurt bad. B-Buckshot."

He made a strange noise in his throat, scratched at his chin again.

"Shotgun, then? Aimed at a lady?"

"I c-couldn't say," Cal managed. "I don't know what happened."

Henry Younts hesitated, not sure if he should go inside, and Cal wondered what was weighing on his mind.

"Your ma in there?" he asked.

Cal nodded.

"With nothin' but Johnny and your gran for help?"

"Yes, sir," he said. "Doc just left."

The preacher blew a breath out while turning towards the house and Cal stood still, the jar suddenly cold in his hands.

"Let's get inside then," Henry Younts said. "I 'spect that young lady needs all the help she can get."

I LAID IN THE STRANGE, narrow bed after Odessa left the room, the blanket pulled up to my neck, wondering why these people would burn all my clothes when the stout woman who seemed mad all the time entered and handed me something that looked like a doily Iris might have used on the arm of her couch.

"You'll be needing this nightdress, then," she said, clearly irritated. "My boy had to get rid of your clothes."

I swallowed, reaching for the garment and she swiveled, fixed me with a stare. "They wasn't fit to be worn out of doors, you know."

"They weren't?" I asked.

"And tell me, what sort of woman goes strolling about in her unmentionables?"

"Unmentionables?" I repeated, trying to remember what I'd been wearing when I'd taken Dylan's hand and stepped onto the Whisper Stone.

"Yes," she said again as I sat up, pulled the nightgown over my head. The next moment I was trying to adjust the strings that were hanging against my neck. "Where did you get such things?"

I squinted, moved to tuck the nightgown under my legs and felt my wounds ignite like a lit firecracker. Three shallow breaths and I remembered my blood-smeared tank top, cut off jean shorts and white tennis shoes. Hardly the stuff dreams were made of, but it seemed to have thrown these people for a serious loop.

"Uh," I said quickly, fiddling with my strings again. "They're all the rage in New York."

"New York?" she asked, stepping forward to tie them herself. "All the rage?"

I nodded.

"Well, I can't say but folks who live there must be dumb as the day is long."

"Excuse me?"

"You say your name is Justine, but some lady named Victoria had her name sewn into your underthings."

I pressed my lips together, tried to suppress my snort of laughter.

"You think that's funny?" she asked. "I wonder what your ma and pa would think of you wandering about in your clothes from New York?"

"Uh-"

"It's not fitting."

"I know."

"Tell me what sort of people are they, then?"

"My folks were killed in a fire downstate," I blurted out, thinking about my real parents, wondering what sort of karma I was racking up. "I was traveling to," I paused, searching for a place she might recognize. "*Mackinac* Island... to be with my boyfriend."

"Your boyfriend?"

I looked at her again, wondering what I'd said wrong.

"You mean your beau?"

I nodded.

"I was sailing up the shore when we were attacked by bandits."

"Bandits?" she asked again, and I chewed on my lip, hoping she would buy it.

"Yes."

"And you were in a boat?" she paused, her small eyes narrowing. "What *boat*?"

I frowned, scared that she would see through my ruse as a picture of a yacht I'd drooled over in the Lantern Creek Marina sprang to mind. Dylan had laughed, saying we could buy one when I finally got that big promotion at Huffs.

"The Wind Gypsy," I mumbled, the memory shaking me.

"Hmmm," she mumbled. "Never heard of it."

I cleared my throat. "They came up beside us, and I jumped overboard. One of them shot at me and I guess... I guess they had good aim."

She sighed, rubbed at her sweaty forehead again. "And what about the others on your boat?"

I shook my head, trying to imagine the scene I was about to create. "I heard screaming. It was terrible,"

She held her hand up, bowed her head and for a moment I thought she was praying. Then her head snapped up again and she put her hands on her hips.

"Your man must be fretting. Johnny will send a letter so he can come fetch you straight away."

I smiled my thanks, my thoughts floating to Dylan and how I

would give my right leg for him to come and 'fetch me straight away.'

Instead, I felt a heaviness building in my heart, amplified by the dark fear that he hadn't gotten through.

And if Henry Younts had hurt him...

I remembered him crouching beneath the shotgun, remembered my brother rushing between and fought to suppress the terror that numbed my skin.

"Did he give you that necklace?" she asked, and I felt my fingers move towards the silver pendant that had become the only constant in my life.

"He has one like it," I said. "It's,"

"A sign of your devotion," she smiled.

I felt my throat tighten.

"Poor thing," the woman said as she patted my hand, the first kindness she'd shown since entering the room. "I know how it feels to miss the man you love."

I looked up at her, milking her sympathy for all it was worth. "You do?"

She nodded. "My Seth has been gone a long time."

"I'm sorry," I said, wondering how this man had fit into the fabric of Cal and Odessa's life.

"Never was a better soul who walked the earth," she smiled, her eyes twinkling. "Aside from your beau, of course. What's his name, dear?"

I smiled, the feel of his name bringing me closer to him.

"Dylan."

She sat down in the chair beside my bed, took the bottle that had been sitting on the nightstand and poured what looked like cough syrup into a spoon.

"And is he handsome, this Dylan of yours?" she asked.

I smiled, thinking that word didn't begin to describe what was beautiful about him.

"Your face tells the tale," she clucked. "You're a pretty little thing so I wouldn't expect any different. We'll be sure to get word out as quick as we can."

"Thank you," I breathed, relief uncoiling my stomach even though her offer was useless.

"But until then, you should take more tonic," she said, and I leaned forward on the bed, eager to dull the edges of the pain that consumed me. "You must always remember that I need the lion's share for my headaches."

I nodded, and the next moment she was feeding me the bitter liquid.

"That's right," she cooed. "You will be feeling better in no time at all."

I settled back against the pillows, pulled the covers up to my chin when a commotion from just behind the closed door caught my attention.

Odessa's voice mingled with Cal's.

And another... deeper, and with a hard edge.

Hot terror electrified my body.

I scrambled backwards on the bed, my feet pushing me towards the headboard, my side exploding in an agony so intense I thought I would pass out.

"What is it?" the woman started as the door creaked open and Odessa squeezed through.

"Justine," she said, her brown eyes large and worried. "Someone is here to see you."

I shook my head, "No... please."

"He is asking to pray over you."

I shook my head again, my fingers gripping the blanket as the door swung open and Henry Younts walked in.

CHAPTER

TWO

"Justine, this is our preacher, Mr. Henry Younts," Odessa tried to calm me, but there was no preparing for the sight as I fought the urge to jump out of bed, grab the nearest gun and blast him into eternity.

Which didn't sound like a bad idea.

"Come now," Odessa's mother tried the sweet approach. "This here's a man of God."

I felt my gaze move towards the large man standing near the foot of my bed and forced myself to look at him.

His eyes were as black as I remembered, his body still hovering well over six feet and close to three hundred pounds as he removed his hat. I looked at his face, expecting to see flesh hanging from bone and was shocked by a hint of color in his cheeks, his bushy eyebrows drawn up in surprise.

As though he didn't know me.

"Justine," Odessa said again. "Will you allow this man to lay hands on you?"

I swallowed. Allow the man who had murdered my father to

touch me? The man who had sent a tree crashing down on Troy and tried to carve up Dylan in the woods beyond Ocqueoc Falls?

I took a deep breath, felt my nostrils flare and gripped the blanket tighter.

"What'd Doc do to her, Louise?" Henry Younts asked. "She seems real skittish."

Cal stepped forward, his brown eyes reminding me of Adam's and in that small likeness I found comfort.

"He gave her a tonic. Must have had too much of Gran's medicine in it."

My eyes flashed to Cal and in them I saw an understanding.

He didn't like this man either.

"All the more reason to get to prayin'," Louise Cook wiped her hands on her apron, ready for business. "This girl needs some rest."

I tensed.

"What happened to you, child?" Henry Younts asked, and I felt my body stiffen, unable to believe he was speaking to me.

I opened my mouth, trying to figure out how to answer him as one human being might another. "I was traveling to Mackinac Island when we were overtaken by bandits."

"Bandits?" he repeated, coming closer, and I felt my knuckles blanch and tightened my shoulders.

"They shot at the men on her boat," Louise added. "We need to get a letter off so her beau can come and fetch her. She can't stay here."

"Hush," Henry bent closer. "That's no way to talk."

I froze, mesmerized by the sight of him, fighting the urge to strike out with everything I had.

"Come, Justine," Odessa moved closer, touching my arm as well.

Cal came next, laid his hand on my shoulder, followed shortly by Louise, who just touched the top of my head.

Then Henry Younts was reaching towards me, his fingers just

brushing my neck and I twisted away, a strange cry coming out of my mouth that did not sound human.

"Saints alive!" Louise shouted. "It seems she has the devil inside of her!"

"Justine," I heard Odessa say, felt her hand tighten on my arm as she fought to control my movements. "You'll open your wound again."

I knew she was right, knew the buckshot could end up killing me before Henry Younts did and still I fought to get away.

"You need to lie still," Henry Younts said, his tone gruff and I felt his words claw through my skin, a sharp pain causing stars to dance before my eyes as I imagined his hands closing around my necklace and ripping it off.

"She's going to faint," Louise said, her voice rising. "Keep her still, girl."

Odessa's hand moved gain, and I knew the strength Butler had given her could easily overpower me. One quick movement and the pain became too much.

I slumped back against the headboard, a sheen of sweat just dusting my skin.

"Child," Henry Younts said, his fingers resting against my shoulder now and I imagined them moving upwards, imagined him squeezing as he had during my vision in Iris' kitchen.

"Please," I said, exhausted and he tightened his hold, his eyes locking with mine and I forced myself to look away, my gaze moving to Cal and in his eyes I saw the fear my actions had caused.

I took a slow breath, succumbed to the fact that if Henry Younts wanted to finish what he'd started, he could easily do it.

"There," Louise said, her tone as soothing as I'd ever heard it. "I do believe the spell has passed."

Henry Younts nodded, then began speaking words under his breath that called for healing and strength and almighty intervention, and I had to admit he had an inclination for it. I felt my body relax in the slightest, tried to remain still as I thought about how easy it would be for this man to end my life here and now.

Or vice versa.

"Amen," he said after the prayer drifted off, each person silently contemplating what had just happened and I felt his hand withdraw, watched as his gaze moved towards Odessa again.

"You have made quite a mess of yourself," Louise scolded. "I am going to insist that Doc find something else to give you."

I nodded, exhausted, and caught sight of her daughter moving into a corner. A moment later Henry Younts followed, and I strained to hear what they were saying even as I clutched the covers to my chin.

He bent his head, his lips moving as his words just reached my ear.

"Wonderin' if you might come to the barn dance out at the Karsten place on Saturday."

My eyes darted to Odessa as I waited on her response, still stunned by the fact that he wasn't trying to kill me.

She smiled in a way I had expected- lovely, kind, thoughtful-, and in that moment I understood why the preacher had hopes she would take his last name.

"Preacher Younts," she said, her voice low, her eyes cutting to her mother, who was pretending to tuck the covers in around the edge of my bed.

"Henry," he said. "I'd be pleased if you called me that."

Her chest rose and fell, then she glanced at me.

"Henry," she began again. "I'm far too busy to go to a dance."

He laughed a little. "Too busy to have a little bit of fun? Come on, Dess,"

Louise started, a small smile painting her lips at the familiar way he had addressed her daughter.

"The farm needs tending to."

"Johnny can tend the farm."

She laughed lightly. "He needs watching over. You know that."

"It's one night, Dess."

"I really couldn't,"

"Please,"

"Henry,"

"For pity's sake, Odessa!" Louise spun on her heel, her wide skirts billowing out. "There's nothing wrong with letting this man take you to a dance. I'm sure we can all work together to have the farm in order by Saturday night."

"Ma," her daughter replied.

Louise approached; her hands balled up into fists on her hips. "I'm telling you to go out and have some fun like young folks is supposed to do."

Odessa shook her head, her eyes cutting to me again. "I don't think,"

"Don't *think* so much, girl! William has been gone a long spell and it's high time you started paying attention to what's in front of you."

I glanced at Odessa as she clasped her hands at her waist, her eyes drifting downwards and knew the confusion she held in her heart.

"Yes, Ma," she said, glancing at the preacher. "I'd be pleased to go to the dance with you."

And then Henry Younts did a thing I didn't believe was possible.

He smiled.

"You will?" he asked, his joy palpable.

Odessa nodded, her eyes on the floor.

"I'll come by in the wagon to fetch you," he said, stumbling over his words as he backed out of the room, and I couldn't help but wonder if his sudden urge to pray over me had more to do with his love life than pastoral duties.

Louise smiled, showed Henry to the front door and I was left alone with the woman I had traveled through time to find.

"Are you feeling better?" she asked, coming towards me. "You gave us a fright and I'm certain it's that tonic-"

"Odessa," I began. "Why did you agree to go to the dance with him?"

She looked up at me, smiled even though I could see unshed tears in her eyes.

"It's as it should be," she said. "Henry Younts is a man of God."

I fought the gasp that bubbled in my throat, unable to believe she'd said those words.

"Are you sure?"

She nodded even as she came over to continue tucking the blanket her mother had left behind. "Of course. But after the way you screamed, I thought he might have to take the devil out of you."

"But" I bit my lip, unsure if I should continue. "You're scared of him. I can see it."

"No."

"Cal is, too."

She shook her head. "Henry Younts has a temper, surely- but what man doesn't?"

"Odessa," I tried again, shifting closer to her even as the pain in my side began to finally subside. "I don't think you should go to the dance."

She laughed. "Why ever not?"

"You have to keep the heart that was given to you," I said, remembering my dream from the summer before and our walk up the steps of Back Forty Farm.

She stopped, drew back for an instant and looked at me.

"What did you say?"

"There's nothing wrong with loving him."

"*Loving* him," she laughed again. "Who are you speaking of?"

"Butler," I said, and Odessa started, her eyes suddenly frightened.

"How do you know him? I asked you before but-"

I opened my mouth, searching for an answer when Louise came rushing back in, her cheeks glowing.

"Well, isn't this just the best bit of news," she clapped her hands together, forgetting for the moment that she had wanted me to rest. "You being escorted into that dance on the arm of Preacher Younts. And at the *Karsten's,* no less! That Penelope has been looking down her nose at us ever since you were with child, and it now seems the dark spot that's been over our family will be washed out."

I watched Odessa's shoulders drop.

"Ma,"

"He's a fine man, Dess."

"Ma," she began again. "I don't,"

Louise turned on her at once, the color high in her cheeks.

"What, Odessa?" she threw her hands up. "Speak!"

She swallowed, uncomfortable.

"I only said yes because you wanted me to. I don't *care* for Preacher Younts in that way."

At once Louise Cook's face changed as she stepped towards her daughter. Then she was gripping the young woman's elbow in a way that must have caused Odessa pain.

"What does it matter what you feel for him?" she said, her voice a hiss. "That no good bastard is gone for good and it's high time you start thinking about your family and what we have suffered. Your pa couldn't take it. His heart gave out."

I watched Odessa's head snap up, her eyes alight with a fire I hadn't seen before.

"Pa died from drink, Ma- and he'd walked a good stretch down that road before Cal ever came along."

I sank lower in the bed.

"You should die of shame for saying that," Louise tightened her grip, her face beet red, her upper lip glistening. "So help me, this better not have to do with that Indian what's staying in the old Rook Cabin."

"Ma,"

"I knew he was sweet on you back when you put in that garden plot, but I thought you had more sense than to take up with him."

"Ma," Odessa twisted in her grasp; her brown eyes large. "You're hurting me."

"If you've taken up with him, Odessa," she stopped, her breath heavy in her chest. "Our family would never live it down. You understand that. *Never...*"

"You know nothing about him."

"Yes I do," her mother said, her hand drawn back as if to strike her daughter and Odessa rose on her toes, gripped her mother's wrist in a way that made her knuckles blanch.

"Let me go."

Louise's face contorted and I knew Odessa was hurting her, knew that this was something unknown to the older woman and that meant the Elk totem had been found.

The next moment Louise was fighting back, pushing her daughter away as she stumbled forward. Odessa went down on one knee, her hands in front of her as Louise turned, ready to hit her across the face.

"Stop!" I cried, and she looked back at me, realizing her mistake.

I threw the covers back, tried to sit up as my wound screamed at me not to move.

"What are you doing?"

The older woman straightened up, patted her hair back in place and tried to slow her heavy breathing. "You just settle down or you're likely to hurt yourself."

I watched Odessa shrink away from her mother, her cheeks ablaze with shame and another, deeper emotion that had taken her by surprise.

"Were you going to hit her?" I asked, barely able to conceal my disgust.

"No," Louise said quickly. "You are mistaken, I'm sure."

I looked at Odessa again, who would not meet my gaze.

"I feel a headache coming on," her mother continued. "I'm going to lie down and rest."

The next moment she was reaching for the bottle on my bedside table, hustling out of the room and I was left alone with Odessa, who looked as though her mother had actually hit her.

"Justine," she began. "I am so sorry."

"Don't say that," I said, suddenly angry. "It wasn't your fault."

She looked at me, dazed, and then pulled her long braid over one shoulder.

"Ma's all fussed up over you being here. She doesn't like the extra work and,"

"It's no excuse."

She looked down at her hands.

"You said you knew about Butler," she paused. "What did you mean?"

I tried to think of a way to explain that I'd traveled back in time on an old Ojibwa petroglyph to steal her precious medicine bag and wipe out the black spot otherwise known as Henry Younts that had been hanging over *our* family for over a century.

"Cal told me," I lied. "When we were coming into the house. He thought he might be able to help me."

Odessa seemed surprised. "He did?"

I nodded.

"Why would you think that I loved him," she asked, her dark eyes holding mine.

"Odessa,"

"It's all very strange."

I shook my head, smiled in the silly way that always threw Dylan off.

"It must be the tonic," I shrugged. "I've had quite a bit, you know."

She paused, looking at me for a beat before Cal stuck his head in the room, a glass jar in his hand.

"Cal," his mother turned. "Did your gran see that?"

He shook his head. "She's asleep in her chair."

Odessa nodded, took the jar from her son, "This will help."

I watched as she placed it on the bedside table, wanting to share the truth even though it would pretty much ruin my chances of finding the medicine bag on my own.

So, I changed the subject.

"You were right to tell your mother about the preacher. She shouldn't expect you to care for that man."

"She has every right to expect it," Odessa corrected. "I brought shame on our family."

Cal moved slightly and my heart burned inside my chest.

At once she turned to him, her brow furrowed.

"Son,"

"It's all right, Ma," he said softly before turning away. "I'll go tend to Lolly and the cow."

Odessa watched as he left, then turned back to me, her eyes filled with questions I wanted desperately to answer.

"Why does everything I do hurt the people I love?" she asked, and I stared at her, wondering the same thing about myself when she moved quietly and shut the door between us.

CHAPTER
THREE

C al heard his gran raise her voice in the next room. The preacher had just gone, a smile on his face so wide a boat could sail through it and it made the boy nervous. If Henry Younts was happy, it was because of something his ma said to him, something *nice,* and he didn't want her to do anything that would make him think of her that way.

He heard the voice rise again and peeked around the corner of the door, the jar of Butler's cherry bark tea in his hand and saw Gran raise her fist. He flinched, knowing he should be used to it by now when Justine threw her covers back.

His gran withdrew, seemed to be sorry.

Or just embarrassed.

He didn't know whether to breathe as she reached for her bottle of laudanum and swept by with an irritated mumble, taking no notice of him in the darkened corner and he sagged against the wall.

Butler had told him to be careful of his gran and Johnny. He'd told him to keep a watch out for the preacher most of all and when

Cal asked, he said he was able to see deep into the hearts of men and Henry Younts had buried his a long time ago.

Cal wondered about it afterwards, had asked his ma and she shook her head, told him about the preacher's wife being thrown from a horse and leaving him with a young son to care for.

"That's why he's so close to God," she said. "He had to depend on him during his most desperate hour."

But Cal didn't think of it that way. It seemed the death of the preacher's wife had done just the opposite, and he didn't want that darkness anywhere near his ma.

He tried to shake the thought, had gone into Justine's room only to hear his ma talk about the shame she'd brought to the family as if he didn't carry the whisper of that burden every day.

Cals stood very still, wanting to go back in time and make things right so his ma could be happy.

But he couldn't, and so he'd gone to see Lolly and stayed for a long while with his face against her neck, his hands clutching her mane before gathering the courage to go inside again.

He'd been on his way to his bed in the loft when he heard Justine call softly to him from her open doorway.

He went to her, saw that she was sitting up in bed and wondered why she wasn't sleeping.

"I'm sorry about what your mother said."

He felt his shoulders tense up even though he knew his ma was asleep in the loft and Gran was snoring in her chair and that Johnny was at the tavern talking about all the strange things that had happened at the farm.

"Did you drink the tea?" he asked.

She shook her head, her pretty eyes that seemed to be all colors at once looking right through him. "I was just about to."

"Here," he took the jar and handed it to her. "The shaman taught me how to make it."

She nodded, reached for it and he saw something on her wrists that matched what he had seen on her knee when Johnny first laid her on the bed. They were scars that had turned white, and Cal remembered seeing the same things on Butler's back when they went swimming in the river.

Cal stared at them a long time before gathering the courage to ask him about them, and Butler didn't scold him like Gran or Johnny would have done. He simply said they were a symbol of a mistake he had made a long time ago and still those lines lingered in Cal's mind, making him wonder what had happened to Justine.

"Did," he began, pointing to them. "Did someone hurt you?"

She turned her wrist over, traced it in a way that made him believe she'd done it before.

"I thought I could protect the people I loved," she said, her voice low. "But I was wrong."

"Adam and Dylan?" he asked, feeling like he shouldn't have said their names, like it might be too much to hear it out loud. "You were calling for them in your sleep."

She looked down, her face shadowed by something that made him sad.

"Yes," she whispered. "I need to find them."

"You asked me about Adam when I found you," he reminded her, his eyes searching hers. "You said he was your brother."

She nodded again, put a hand to her cheek and held it there. "You look like him. And I thought for a minute..."

Cal stood still, feeling sorry for her again and so he handed her the jar, watched as she took a long drink, the muscles in her throat working as she swallowed the liquid.

"How could those scars protect anyone?" he asked after she had finished, and she frowned, reminding him of his ma.

"I'll tell you someday," she said. "I promise, Cal."

He watched her again, feeling like she would keep her word.

"I'm sorry about what you saw" Cal said suddenly, not knowing why.

She looked unhappy again, her large eyes shadowed. "Has your grandmother done that before?"

He glanced at the open door, looked to the chair where Louise continued to sleep.

"Gran hasn't been the same since Grandpa died. Pa ran off just before and she," he shook his head, unable to believe the words that were pouring from his mouth, words he'd been longing to say for so long now revealed to a stranger.

But she didn't feel like one.

"She blames my ma. Blames her for having me."

"No, Cal,"Justine said quickly. "You can't think of it that way."

He looked at her long and hard.

"I know my coming into the world was a sin. I know Gran wants Preacher Younts to marry Ma so people will stop talking about us."

"No

"I want that, too."

She stopped, pulled on the inside of her mouth with her teeth. "Has your ma ever... fought back like that?"

Cal felt his neck get hot, remembering how the shaman had told him strength would begin to reveal itself after they found the Elk antler on the edge of a large field that sat beside the Big Lake.

"No," he said, unable to lie. "Ma has always been afraid of Gran."

"Why?" she asked, and Cal took a step backwards, uncomfortable with what he had said.

"I gotta go. I already told you too much."

He watched Justine's hands tighten on the blanket and felt bad because maybe her curiosity was only because she was lonely and wanted to talk.

"I'll help Uncle Johnny send that letter off tomorrow," he said, hoping to comfort her. "Then you can be movin' on."

The girl looked down for a moment, hurt in her eyes and Cal felt bad again. He didn't want to make her feel that way, but he couldn't be talking to her like he was- didn't understand why she wanted to know all these things in the first place.

"Thank you," she said, her voice a whisper. "I'm already starting to feel better."

The boy smiled.

"I knew the tea would work. There's some salve Butler made hidden in the shed, too. I'll bring it up in the morning when Gran hangs the wash."

The girl looked at him, her large eyes wanting to know things again.

"Why do you have to hide things from her?" she asked.

Cal took a step back, that feeling again in the pit of his stomach that switched between wanting to stay and run away.

"She don't like the shaman and Uncle Johnny just does what she tells him. They think the things he does is wicked an' they know..." he stopped. "They know he's sweet on my ma."

Justine smiled and Cal felt his heart stop.

"You can't tell no one, Miss. I'll get the strap for sure and won't walk for a week."

She reached her hand out and he went to her as easily as a friend.

"I'll never hurt you, Cal," she paused. "I promise."

"Miss,"

"I'm here to help you."

"You're here because you're hurt," he corrected, her blood-soaked bandages visible through her white nightgown. "And I have something for that."

She looked at him, questioning, and he reached into his pocket, pulled out a burlap sack tied off with string.

He remembered the moment Butler gave it to him, remembered his promise to keep it safe with the antler and Cal had no idea why he was showing it to Justine other than the strange feeling he'd been having in her presence.

"What is it?" she asked, leaning forward and Cal could see the discomfort that simple movement caused her.

Untying the top of the burlap bag, he shook the contents into his hand.

"It's a snakeskin," he said. "I keep it safe under the floorboard in that corner."

"Cal," she whispered, her face suddenly white.

"It'll heal you," he said. "Butler says so."

"Heal me?" she said, her voice so low he could hardly hear it.

"Can I trust you?" he asked, unsure why he'd asked such a silly question because there was no way of knowing whether he could trust someone he'd just met.

"Of course," she whispered; her eyes locked on the object in his hand. Then she looked up, smiled again. "What would I want with an old snakeskin anyway?"

Cal took a deep breath, his mind in a free-fall, and placed it in her hand.

CHAPTER

FOUR

I lay in the darkness after Cal left me, alone in a strange house in an even stranger time that held nothing for me besides a consuming desire to accomplish what I had come to do.

I considered my options, one being a scenario where I took the snakeskin and burnt it. And still I wondered if the destruction of this totem would end the curse that had tormented me for the past year. I wasn't sure how the medicine worked and hadn't exactly come up with a foolproof plan when I'd made the rash decision to come here.

I adjusted the blankets, said a small prayer for the healing power of the cherry bark tea, which had allowed me to think clearly for the first time since I'd been shot.

I reached beside my pillow, felt the burlap pouch with my fingertips and wondered where the other totems were.

I knew Odessa and her mother shared this room and wondered where a suitable hiding place might be.

A pine dresser stood against the far wall, and I stopped breathing, listened for movement on the other side of the closed door.

Hearing nothing, I sat up carefully and swung my legs over the side of the bed.

Pain radiated down my hip and through my leg and still I stood, gritting my teeth as I gripped the bedpost.

A minute passed, the pain beginning to subside as I took a step towards the dresser. Seven steps later and I pulled out a drawer, shoving clothing aside before realizing Odessa was too smart to hide the medicine bag where Louise might find it. And still, my lifelong love of snooping had me running my fingers over the strange fabric, wondering how much time and care had gone into making each piece.

No wonder they had set fire to my tank top and shorts.

Moving away, I went slowly to my knees and looked under the bed. Nothing was there except a pile of quilts that had probably taken longer to make than anything I'd attempted to do in my life.

I stood up straight, my hope faltering as I turned in a slow circle. A rifle hung on two pegs above the door.

Henry Younts had been so close to me, had put his hands on me and prayed over me, his words casting an uncommon light on the dark corners of my heart.

I looked at the gun again.

All I had to do was grab it, make my way to his house and put the muzzle against his head.

It was so simple.

I took a step forward and reached up, listening again for any sound that would suggest someone in the household was awake.

All was silent, which meant the world slumbered on and my victim might be, too.

I stood on tiptoe and lifted the rifle off its pegs.

Once in my hands, I examined it, wondering if I could use it. The weapon was long and sleek, with a dark wooden stock and metal hammer. I knew how to shoot, had watched enough movies to know that pioneers always kept their guns loaded which meant

Henry Younts would likely meet the Maker he'd been avoiding once I figured out how to pull the trigger.

I crept to the front door and opened it quietly, the evening air filling my lungs as I slipped outside. Creeping across the lawn, I felt like a ghost in my white nightgown, my hair spilling over my shoulders as the moon sailed a cloudy sea.

I stood for a moment, wondering which way to go, thinking that most preachers lived close to their churches and that if I could just get down to the river, I would probably find the church somewhere along its banks.

I paused, Jamie Stoddard's face coming to mind. I hoped he had made a home elsewhere so I wouldn't have to explain why I'd murdered his father in front of him.

I imagined tossing the rifle aside after the deed was done and running towards the woods, hopeful I could find the Whisper Stone and get back home to the people I loved.

But what would be waiting once I got there?

Would Troy be standing in the same place I'd left him with Amanda and Pam? Where would my brother be, or the man I loved?

Would they know who I was, or had killing the preacher destroyed the reason we'd come together in the first place?

I stopped cold, fear clamping around my heart when I remembered what Dylan had said.

Anything could change the future, could change us, could change Adam...

I pulled in a breath, wishing he were here to help me. He would be logical and precise, pushing emotion aside to reach a rational conclusion and if I could just hang on long enough, he might find me and then-

"Miss Justine!" a voice from just ahead startled me and I stopped, took a stumbling step backwards in the darkness.

The next moment Johnny Cook came into view, his pale eyes shining like silver dollars in the moonlight.

"What in the world are you doin' out of bed? And this far from the house?"

"Uh," I murmured, shocked to see him here in the dark, wondering how I would explain the rifle in my hands.

"You shouldn't be out here alone."

'I'm sorry," I stood up straighter, tried to regain my composure. "I thought I heard something."

"Why're you handlin' that gun?" he asked, his head cocked to the side, and I wondered if he was trying to make sense of what he had seen. "Do you know how to shoot?"

"I-," I began again. "I *do* know how to shoot. Have since I was a little girl."

He put one hand on his hip, touched the revolver that hung there. "That so?"

I tightened my grip on the rifle, ready to use it against anything I saw as a threat, but then he grinned, a strange thing that made me understand why Louise had pinned all her hopes on Odessa.

"I 'spect you might be confused on account of that tonic."

"No," I protested. "I'm perfectly fine. And I know what I heard."

"Settle down, now," he said, his smile going slack. "It was most likely a critter looking for a midnight snack. This wood is full o' bear and wolves and other things that hunt at night."

I tightened my grip, wondering what would have happened if I'd run into something that could kill me aside from Henry Younts.

"Did you come from the tavern?" I asked. "I thought the preacher said he was going that way after he left the house."

He nodded his head. "Yes, ma'am. But Preacher wasn't there. His place sits up past the sawmill. Tavern's the other way, down by the livery stable."

"Oh?" I asked, watching him point off in the darkness.

"I'll take you up to look around when you're feeling better."

I smiled in a way I thought might be charming.

"I'd like that very much."

He grinned again, a distant thing that held no meaning and then shifted his weight, held out his hand.

"I'll take that rifle now."

I felt myself stiffen, thinking again of the totems hidden inside the medicine bag, the anger that had fueled my strength lighting my senses.

I imagined swinging the stock upwards and catching him in the face, imagined him falling into the grass while I ran away towards the little house by the sawmill.

"Johnny," I warned, my voice low. "I think I need to keep looking for what I heard. It could come to the house and go after Lolly and the cow."

He laughed then. "You are overwrought, I 'spect, and Lolly and that cow are safe inside good, thick walls."

He reached forward- his large, clumsy hand closing around the barrel, and I pulled back, expecting the gun to break free but he held it fast.

I pulled back again and felt my breath catch in my throat. Odessa had shown unusual strength earlier that evening, making me believe the Elk totem had been found. I tightened my grip, my knuckles blanching and wondered why the medicine wasn't working.

"Time to go," Johnny said.

I glanced down at the hands that had knocked Stumpy off his barstool and lifted a tree from Troy Phillips' back and had no idea who I was.

"Come now," he said in his slow, sing-songy voice and I uncurled my fingers, allowing him to take the rifle because there was nothing more I could do.

"That's good," he said, the sight of the house and a single lantern burning in the window calling us home. I glanced at the woods, heard the wind rustling through the tops of the tall pines and saw something glimmer in the moonlight.

"Johnny," I whispered, my hand on his arm. "Something's out there."

He stopped, glanced over his shoulder, and then turned quickly. There, in the darkness on the edge of the tree line a pair of eyes shone in the moonlight. I felt my shoulders tense and clamped my jaw together. The animal was standing still, his gray fur just visible as it blew in the breeze.

"It's a wolf," Johnny said, his voice low. "A pack of 'em has been hunting on the other side of the field."

"A wolf?" I repeated, my heart speeding up. I'd never been close to one before, but it didn't move, didn't approach us as Johnny raised the rifle.

"I've never seen this one," he said, holding the butt against his shoulder and something inside me wanted him to stop.

"Johnny," I began.

"Wonder where he came from."

I didn't know how to answer him, but stood transfixed as he watched the wolf, his clear eyes widening for just a moment before the moon sailed behind a cloud, plunging us into darkness.

"Dammit," he cursed, and I grabbed hold of his arm.

"What do we do?"

"He might be circling 'round to join his pack. We'd best get to the house before they cut us off."

I nodded, grateful that Johnny was here even as my senses came alive in the night. The wolf was here, watching us from some shadowy corner and I should have been terrified.

But I wasn't.

I followed Johnny closely, peering over my shoulder as we closed the distance to the house. Once on the porch, he opened the door and I stood for a moment, watching the moon as it reappeared.

The tree line was empty.

"I 'spect that critter knew he couldn't make a meal of us,"

Johnny smiled. "You were good to listen quick or we might've been in a world of hurt."

"Yes," I said, more to myself than him as I went inside. Once there, I stood in the center of the room, listening to Louise snore from her chair as Johnny laid the rifle on the table, turning to me once he did.

"I told the men in town about how those bandits shot at you."

"You did?" I said mildly.

He frowned. "Old Jeb Price lives near the Big Lake and was outside workin' on his woodpile most of the day. Said everything was calm and quiet," another pause. "Where did you say you were?"

"Oh," I began, fear beginning to rise in my chest. "I think it was the Old Presque Isle Lighthouse."

"Presque Isle," he blinked- looked at me for a moment and then blinked again. "Miss Ebersole likes to take air out there sometimes. Maybe she heard something."

"Miss Ebersole?" I repeated, thinking of the beautiful woman whose death had created the mess I was knee deep in.

Johnny nodded again. "Lives out at the Back Forty Homestead with her husband. Says the lake air is good for her since she took sick."

I frowned, unaware that Esther Ebersole had been in anything but perfect health before her husband shot her.

"Well, I'll just be heading to bed now, Miss Justine. I'm glad you're feelin' better."

"Thank you," I said, anxious for him to go, wondering what I would do once he climbed into the loft to lay beside his sister and her son.

One glance over his shoulder and he grabbed the rifle.

I looked at him, suddenly guilty and he smiled his strange smile again before climbing the ladder and I walked slowly to my room.

A minute passed, then another. I still stood, unable to get back into bed.

I'd failed to kill Henry Younts, failed to destroy the snakeskin, and still questioned whether either would get me what I wanted.

I went to the window and looked out into the night, thinking of the wolf again, wondering how far it had come and if it knew I was hunting as well.

I remembered how the totems had looked in my hand the first time I held them- the turtle shell and black feather, the white antler and jawbone.

I reached over, turned the kerosene lamp down and found myself in darkness again.

But I was not alone.

Against the tree line, the eye shine watched me back.

* * *

It was later that night that I dreamt of the silver canoe.

My father sat in the stern, his back straight and sure, his paddle across the gunwales as he had been before. To his right, a willow kissed its mirror image, and I went to the river, felt the water touch my toes.

Over his shoulder and on the other bank, the wolf stood watching, his gray fur ruffled by the wind.

I looked down and saw the jawbone at my feet.

"J," a voice said, one that seemed familiar.

I raised my eyes, the man I loved standing where my father had been.

"Dylan," I whispered, feeling like I was pulling on a thread that could unravel at any moment as I rushed into the water and into his arms.

"Where's Adam?" I choked; not sure I wanted the truth.

"Troy's taking care of him."

I felt the heaviness lift from my chest, knowing he would protect my brother with his life.

"Where are you?"

"I'm trying to find you," he said, his hands tangling in my hair as he pressed his lips to my forehead.

"I'm with Odessa," I said, hopeful he would find me. "I found her, Dylan. I found all of them."

I felt his arms tighten, knew he was listening and realized this constant, steady reassurance was what I missed the most.

"I knew you would."

I laughed, "That makes one of us."

I heard him chuckle, his fingers reaching for my necklace.

"You know what they say about this," he said, touching the silver circle, moving the pendant until it met the clasp, and I was reminded of my friends gathered in the hallway of Webber Middle School, Jake Jones catching my eye through the cafeteria window.

"It means someone is thinking of you," I smiled, loving the way I felt when we were together.

"It's true," he said, as he pulled me closer, his index finger lifting my chin until my lips touched his.

"Dylan," I whispered, wanting to share my thoughts with him. "Henry Younts doesn't know who I am. And if I could just get a gun,"

He pulled back, his eyes darkening. "He could kill you."

I shook my head. "He'd never hear me; never even know I was there and then I could come back to you and Adam."

He paused. "Could you?"

I looked at him, wondering what he meant as the water began to rise to our knees.

"Don't do it, J."

"But" I stumbled over the word, wanting to keep him with me, terrified that he would be taken away. "What do I do?"

"Stay alive," he said, the water up to our waist now and I clung to him as the current began to pull us apart.

"*Please,*"

"Promise me."

I nodded, reaching for him as the water lifted me from my feet, carrying me down river as the wolf kept pace on the other side of the bank.

"Dylan," I gasped, coarse blankets grasping my ankles as the current had moments before and I opened my eyes, the empty room before me and felt my mind spiral to a place it had never been before.

I buried my face in my pillow and screamed at my brother in silent agony.

WHERE ARE YOU?

I listened, heard the breeze break away from the windowpane and felt a sob wrack my chest.

DON'T LEAVE ME HERE.

I listened again, and as the quiet took hold of my heart, I thought of Johnny Cook and how he had taken the rifle from me.

I squeezed my eyes shut, imagining for a moment that I had turned the gun on myself.

Stay alive...

I felt his words spark something inside of me and reached for my necklace, felt the circle intersected with the cross, and just beside it...

I touched the clasp, felt hope lift my heart.

You know what they say about this...

I closed my eyes, felt tears building and covered my mouth with my hand, praying I could keep my promise.

CHAPTER
FIVE

"You look a sight better than the last time I saw you," Louise Cook barked in her usual manner as she looked me up and down.

Three days had passed since my dream and here I stood in the middle of the bedroom, Odessa before me as she tucked in the side of the blue dress she'd been altering, a sewing needle in her mouth.

"That your old one, Dess?" her mother asked, and the girl nodded, her eyes sparkling in a way that said she was pleased with her work.

I looked in the mirror, thought about how far I'd come in such a short time, and smiled.

"Don't fool with this nonsense for long," Louise ordered. "Dinner needs tending to."

"Yes, Ma," her daughter nodded.

Doc had been by earlier to change my bandages and then had gone outside to talk with Johnny. I had been surprised at how young he was, how awkward he seemed when I assumed he'd cleaned his fair share of wounds before.

"I've been to this house more than I'd like in the past few

months," he said while looking at Odessa. "Although I don't mind helping a lady after such an unfortunate incident. Your beau must be very worried."

I'd shifted on the bed, uncomfortable to be talking about Dylan while this man had his hands on me.

"Yes," I said, my voice low. "I'm hoping we are reunited soon."

"How long have you been apart?" he asked, his brown hair slicked back from his face, his glasses resting on the bridge of his nose in a way that made him look studious.

I took a breath, tired of repeating my lies but knowing I couldn't stop now. "Almost a year."

He shook his head. "A long time to be separated from a woman such as yourself."

I swallowed; my face red as he finished wrapping the cloth around my waist.

Later, after the young doctor had gone, I'd asked Odessa about it.

"Doc's looking for a wife," she smiled, the color high in her cheeks, making me wonder if his recent house calls had been necessary. "Has been for awhile now."

"Your mother should be pleased," I smiled, and Odessa shook her head.

"Ma doesn't put much stock in schooling. She thinks a good man must get his hands dirty during the week and then wash up on Sunday."

I laughed as I turned in front of the mirror. "She's right."

"If you ask me," Odessa said while tucking in the last of the extra folds and securing them with straight pins. "I think Phineas Marchand needs to go dunk his head in a tub of cold water."

"Marchand?" I asked, biting my lip to keep from laughing, thinking I might have to give Holly a hard time about following in her ancestor's hot to trot footsteps.

I suppressed a smile, memories of gossiping while the boys grilled burgers on the back deck making me homesick.

I imagined our Friday night Euchre games, Salmon Fest and the familiar road that led to Three Fires and Huffs.

I saw myself ducking beneath the slapdash string of Christmas lights, Mallard holding court while Reba McIntyre sang about a girl named Fancy and had to admit I missed the place more than I ever thought I would.

"You're smiling," Odessa said, her brown eyes seeking mine in the mirror.

I met her gaze, a strange feeling overtaking me as I touched my necklace again. "I was just thinking about home."

Odessa smiled, pulled on my skirt while checking the length. "And where is that?"

I felt my heart speed up in the slightest, wondering what I should say. "A little town called Webber. Just south of..." I paused, hoping like hell the place existed. "Kalamazoo."

She nodded, pulled on the skirt again.

"I suppose it's lovely there," she said, continuing to touch the fabric of my dress as though looking for something she could improve upon. "You must think we're hopelessly unrefined."

"No," I stammered.

"You having clothes from New York, and all,"

"What?" I repeated, my mind drawing a blank.

She stopped, looked at me. "The clothes Johnny burned. Ma said they were from New York."

"Oh, yes," I said quickly. "Yes, they were."

She stared at me for a moment, her sharp mind chewing hard on something, and I knew I had to distract her.

"When Doc said he'd been out here more often than he liked, what did that mean?"

She glanced up quickly and shook her head, "He came to tend to Cal when he took sick from eating the spotty melons and then when Johnny broke his arm."

I nodded. I knew about the spotty melons. But there was something more.

"Odessa,"

She stood up, smoothed her dress. "Ma's temper changed after Pa died. That's when she started getting her headaches."

I nodded again, thinking of that upraised hand and the way Odessa had cowered before it.

"How did Johnny break his arm?" I asked, wondering if I wanted to hear the truth.

My grandmother took a quick breath. "Farm work and such." One quick glance at me and I knew she was lying, just as I knew the deception bothered her.

"You must have had a hard time keeping up while he was hurt."

She nodded, tucked a stray piece of hair behind her ear. "Butler came by for a spell and that made a difference."

I tried not to smile. "I'm sure it did."

"Ma wasn't happy about it. She got angry with me one night and..." she stopped again. "I got in her way. Doc came by to make sure I was all right."

I looked at her, wanting to tell her what I really thought of the little tyrant strutting around the house, and bit my tongue.

"She got angry with you because you're friends with Butler?"

The young woman looked down.

"I know it's not fitting, but he's so kind to me. "

"You deserve to be treated that way."

"Pa took sick after Cal's father left us. It shamed the family and now Ma gets upset over the smallest things."

"Odessa," I said, aware of the thin line I was walking. "Nothing gives her the right to hit you, especially not loving a man who loves you back."

She shook her head, color rising to her cheeks.

"I don't love him. Where did you get such a notion?"

"Odessa,"

"Being grateful to someone is one thing, loving them is quite another."

"Please,"

"Cal likes you and because of that I suspect he has let his tongue wag," she said, her eyes hard for just a moment. "Am I right?"

I looked down, the naughty child feeling in full effect again when she shook her head, busied herself by gathering up the items for her sewing basket.

"I will have to tell him to watch what he says."

"No," I said, hoping I hadn't gotten him in trouble.

"I'll talk to him later," she said, clearly trying to change the subject. "But now we must hurry because Ma insists I take you to market."

"Market?" I repeated, feeling dumb.

"She wants you to start helping around the house," she said. "Do you cook?"

"Oh,"I stammered, thinking of the miserable excuse for hamburgers I used to fry up at Huffs. "I wouldn't say I really know *how* to-"

"Never you mind," she smiled, the old Odessa back. "Ma would eat a dead horse if someone said Penelope Karsten was doing the same."

I pressed my lips together.

"She's anxious to show you off is all," she said. "It's been a while since our family's had something to brag about."

I smiled, thinking of the events to come, wondering how the family would be remembered afterwards.

"I'll teach you a few chores, "she said. "Ma has no need for things that are not useful."

I felt a strange tug deep in my belly and gave a half smile, content to play along when there came a knock at the front door.

"There she is!"

I looked to her, questioning and Odessa put her hands together as though she was excited.

"I invited someone to walk to market with us today."

"You did?" I asked, following her into the next room.

"She's lost her family as well," she said, pausing at the door now, her hand on the knob. "And has worked on the Ebersole homestead since early spring."

I sucked in my breath, the mention of Back Forty Farm sending a jolt through me.

"Who is it?" I asked, already knowing the answer as Odessa opened the door and Sara Bennett walked in.

CHAPTER

SIX

Cal knew it was market day, knew his ma and gran would be busy buying and preparing food for the week. He also knew it was his best chance to see Ana Cuppy again. With all the fuss over Justine being there, he hadn't been to school in the last few days.

His ma's eyes had sparkled when he told her about meeting Ana, like she knew something that he didn't. And then a shadow had passed over her face, like she was remembering something and Cal knew what it was because all bad things began and ended with his pa.

Which was why he liked the shaman so much.

His ma had smiled more since spring than ever before, and even though Gran and Johnny disapproved, he didn't care. His ma was happy, and that's all that mattered.

"Don't be gone long, Calvert Cook," she had scolded, a playful tint to her voice. "Johnny will be wanting your help in the fields today."

He nodded, hopeful he would have time to see Butler first.

He watched from the window as his ma and Justine and Sara

Bennett started the long walk to town, each carrying a basket while his gran trailed behind atop Lolly.

He scanned the yard for his uncle and didn't see him.

He glanced at the three women again and was reminded of how much Justine looked like his ma, a thing that had scared him when he first saw her lying in the field.

He thought about her beau, wondering how it would feel when he took her back to Mackinac Island, wondering if he would miss her.

Knowing he would.

He looked out the window for his uncle again, saw him in the fields, walking the edge rows of corn, the chilled air promising an early harvest and an end to his wanderings in the woods.

He opened the door, squeezed his tanned and callused feet into a pair of shoes he hadn't worn since April and took off towards the woods and the little cabin tucked in the arms of a myrtle-covered hill- birch and cedar standing guard not far from the front door.

Cal ran, not knowing if Butler would be at the Rook Cabin- so named because a man called Rook had built it for his wife, abandoning it when she died of sickness.

No one had wanted to live there since his sudden departure, the women fearing the place still carried disease, the men doing what the women wanted. Then Butler had come to town, taken one look at his ma and settled in where no one else would.

Cal passed through a valley, knowing the cabin was just over the next rise and felt his heart speed up like it always did when he was going to meet the shaman, recognizing it as excitement tempered by fear.

Butler told him he wanted to teach him the things that his father and grandfather had taught him beside the fires of his people, and Cal wanted the same thing. His only worry was that he wouldn't learn fast enough or know what to do when the time came to do something really important.

But the shaman told him not to fret, the knowledge was already inside of him just waiting to be woken up.

His movement flushed out a doe, and as she ran towards the river, Cal slowed down. He didn't want to startle Butler although he could think of nothing that would scare the shaman besides losing his ma.

He crested the hill and saw the little gray cabin with its window placed neatly beside the door, smoke rising from the chimney and that meant Butler was home.

He stopped just short of the yard, gave the call of the whip-poorwill, and waited.

Cal bent down on his haunches, thinking of the time he'd gotten sick on the spotty melons, how Doc had thought he might not get better. He remembered Penelope Karsten's daughter, Abigail, coming to tend to him, her bright eyes reminding him of an angel.

He had been lying in bed, thinking he might die when the shaman appeared. He remembered Abigail standing up, offering him her place and he had taken it.

Butler had healed him that day, had given him some strange mixture of tonics he'd made from things found in the woods, had placed his hands on the boy and said words he didn't understand. It was only later he learned how Abigail had kept Gran occupied in the orchard until Butler was able to sneak away.

He made the call of the whippoorwill again.

The door opened.

A man stepped out, lean and well-muscled from years of living off the land, his long hair tied back with a piece of rawhide, his dark eyes searching for Cal.

The boy stood up and the shaman smiled, his face transformed.

"Oshkinawe," he said, using the name he had given Cal from his own language, a name reserved for a boy who was becoming a man.

"Nibwaakaa," he replied, giving honor to his status as a carrier of wisdom.

They walked towards each other, Butler clapping the boy on the shoulder, speaking to the bond they had formed over a summer spent in the forgotten corners of the forest.

"Where is your mother," he asked, his eyes seeking the path behind him, perhaps hoping for a glimpse of her and Cal wondered if she had ever come here alone.

She'd visited with Cal once before and sat in a chair by the fire, her hands folded in her lap, listening to the shaman speak about plants and animals and how they could be used to heal the sick. She had been very still, her large eyes watching the man in front of her, listening to every word until she stood suddenly and walked out the door.

The shaman motioned for Cal to stay inside, had gone after her and at once the boy went to the window and looked out. At first, he saw nothing, but then a sudden movement caught his eye. His ma, in the same dress she'd given to Justine, stood at the edge of the clearing, her back to Butler as he put his hands on her shoulders.

His ma started, and Cal had thought about yelling for him to leave her alone even as something in the shaman's touch said he meant no harm.

Cal watched the shaman slowly turn his ma around, watched as he touched her cheek, taking her long braid and running his thumb along the length of it.

He watched his ma rise on her toes, her lips seeking his and Cal stumbled backwards, knocking over a chair. Quickly he picked it up, his heart racing with fear and something else that surprised him.

He was sitting where they left him when they came back inside, the color high in his ma's cheeks. Butler had gone on talking, his ma listening but when she looked at him again there was a light in her eyes that said something had changed.

"She went to market with the new gal that's staying with us,"

Cal answered, his words bringing him back to the present moment and Butler nodded, stepping aside so he could enter the cabin.

"Look on the table," he said once they were inside.

The boy did as he was told, saw something white and moved to get a closer look.

It was a jawbone, three canines still attached, and Cal imagined the old wolf lying down in a quiet spot to rest, his body returning slowly to the earth as one season wore into the next.

"Is this," Cal asked, his finger reaching out before he could stop it. "Is this for Ma?"

Butler nodded. "Does she still have the bag I made for her?"

"Yes," Cal said. "She keeps it hid with her special things."

The shaman smiled.

"And you gave her the shell and the snakeskin?" he asked, and Cal nodded, remembering the morning he had taken the snakeskin back from Justine, half surprised that she had slept beside it all night.

"These are the last of the totems," Butler said. "The medicine is now complete. You must take this to your mother and keep it with the others. When the moon is full, I will show you what to do next."

Cal nodded again, feeling like the moment had come when everything would finally be as it should.

"You will be protected, Oshkinawe. No harm will ever come to you no matter what happens to me."

Cal frowned. He had always thought the shaman would be the one looking out for them, not a bunch of totems in a medicine bag.

"Are you going away?" he asked suddenly, afraid of what he was thinking.

Butler came to him, placed a hand on his shoulder.

"I will never leave you. My spirit will always guide you in the way that you must go."

Cal looked down, his heart speeding up when he thought about what Butler had said.

"Your ma did a foolish thing when she told fortunes for the women at church."

"Nibwaakaa,"

"She was just beginning to feel her power, to see things that had remained hidden and she was quick to use it, quick to please those who had been cruel to her."

Cal nodded, knowing it was true.

"True wisdom comes slowly. And with much patience."

Cal thought back again to that terrible day, how his Uncle Johnny had sent for Gran, how she had come from Sister Nan's house as soon as she heard, giving his ma the beating of her life when she got home.

"I know," the boy admitted, remembering her blackened eye and swollen lip. "My gran,"

"I know what she did, Oshkinawe," he paused, his eyes thoughtful in the night. "Your mother came to me that night and I... I healed her."

"You did?" Cal asked, wondering what that meant.

"But this," he touched the jawbone with the tip of his finger. "Will give her the strength to fight back. Your grandmother will never hurt her again."

Cal blinked hard, the tears he always fought to suppress tickling his nose.

"Nibwaakaa,"

"Come," he said, taking the totem, moving towards the door. "We have no time to lose. Our long summer days are over. Your uncle will need you in the fields and there is one last thing we need to do."

"Where are we going?" the boy asked, thinking of Ana Cuppy, her brown eyes promising something even the shaman couldn't give.

"The wind is stirring, telling me of things that have not yet come to pass. Their voices are carried on the eagle's wings, and I hear them at night, searching for the totems."

"You mean," the boy swallowed. "Someone wants them?"

Butler nodded and Cal felt gooseflesh rise on his arms.

"Who is it?" he asked, wondering if he had mistakenly told someone and thought of Ana again as they held hands behind the schoolhouse. Had he looked into her eyes and told her his secret to make himself seem stronger, the only apprentice of a powerful shaman?

"I do not know," Butler replied. "It is hidden from me."

Cal stood, waiting for him to explain.

"But we will ask the ancestors. They have helped the Midewiwin before."

"Ancestors?" Cal repeated, thinking of his Uncle Johnny and grandfather- the men who were supposed to guide him and looked up at the shaman. "Midewiwin?"

"They protect a secret place," he said. "A sacred place."

"Where?" Cal asked, following behind as a wind came from the north, bringing with it the scent of winter.

The shaman turned, his voice low and sure.

"The Whisper Stone."

CHAPTER
SEVEN

I tried to keep pace with Odessa as we made our way towards the market, Louise plodding along on Lolly as the woman Dylan had kissed three days ago walked beside me.

I stole a glance at her and knew by the way she held her hands over her stomach that the baby who would one day become Amanda Bennett was growing inside of her.

I thought about Troy and the dream he had of building her a cabin on the banks of the Au Train River and felt a lump rise in my throat.

I stopped, distracted by the thought and the pain in my feet as I rotated my ankle, wishing for my adored pink flip flops and the man who had dared me to walk home in them.

"Are you alright?" Odessa asked.

I nodded, pushing my hair back from my face as it fell from the braid Odessa had so carefully plaited before we left.

"My shoes," I said as Louise rode past me, her face pinched as she shook her head.

Just that morning I'd crammed my feet into a pair of high-topped boots Cal had dug up and my toes were paying the price.

Odessa put a hand to her lips to hide her smile. "They fit me before Cal was born. I suspect they are a bit tight."

I wanted to pinch her for making fun of me but knew that wouldn't put me on the fast track to finding the totems.

"Do you have anything bigger?"

"Sara might," Odessa said while turning to the woman I'd been unable to say more than two words to. "She has *three* pair because she's Esther's pet. Can you even imagine?"

I laughed, glancing nervously at Sara.

"I am only spoiled because Abraham does the same for her."

"Oh?" Odessa said, her mood light. "And how do you know that?"

"She has her pick of his horses," she asked. "And entertains whenever he happens to be away, which is often these days. Although it does help take her mind off things."

"Sara," Odessa said again, "Justine has only arrived, and I don't think,"

"Although that young timber jack also distracts her."

"*Sara*," Odessa whispered, trying to silence her but she laughed again, waved her hand as though airing her mistress's dirty laundry was just a normal part of her day.

"I do wonder if he will steal a dance tomorrow night although it would not be fitting, being the preacher's son and all-"

"Jonas!" I said before I could stop myself.

"My goodness," Sara stopped in her tracks. "How in the world did you know that?"

Odessa looked at me, wondering the same thing and I fought for a thought, *any* thought that would seem plausible. "Johnny mentioned him yesterday. Said he came out and split wood for the winter and did a poor job of it."

Odessa and Sara looked at each other.

"I thought Cal cut up that wood," my grandmother said.

I felt my mouth go dry. "Nope! It was Jonas Younts. I'm sure of it."

"*Nope*," Odessa shook her head. "Is that how they talk in Webber?"

I heard Sara laugh as she waved her hand again.

"Well, I don't care who split the wood, I just know that timber jack has been finding all sorts of reasons to come by. Why, Esther has only to crook her little finger and,"

I heard Odessa clear her throat, saw her glance at me again as Sara's cheeks turned red, perhaps realizing at last the trouble she could cause.

"People tell me I talk too much," she sighed, as far from the unhinged woman I'd known in Lantern Creek as was humanly possible, and it made me realize what the loss of Andrew Karsten had done to her.

I pushed that thought from my mind, trying not to analyze how bending the space time continuum might affect *my* mental state as the road widened.

I felt Odessa grab my arm, anxious to introduce me to the townspeople. I put on a brave face as she explained what was about to happen.

Because cold weather had set in, people were gathering in Mr. Jennison's barn, which was just on the outskirts of town near the tavern Johnny frequented. Those who wanted to make some money or to barter for goods brought what they could spare from their household, while those who were in short supply came to purchase.

I looked at my empty basket and felt embarrassment creep in, knowing the Cook family had faced their fair share of hardship this year.

Odessa noticed my mood.

"The garden didn't take like we had hoped," she said. "Next year will be different."

I looked into her eyes, felt the strength that had allowed her to survive even as a smattering of buildings appeared in front of me.

I frowned, trying to connect this odd assembly of structures to the town I loved and couldn't get my bearings. The woods were too deep, the Big Lake too distant as I glanced down the dusty road, wondering if it was the same one I'd driven to town on.

I thought of Holly, felt a strange tingle beneath my nose and knew I'd give anything for a bit of her sarcasm right now. She'd know just what to say to make the situation better, or at least bearable, and I needed someone who knew who I really was, so I didn't have to keep lying and pretending and-

"People are very curious about you," Odessa's voice startled me. I looked at her, Sara standing expectantly.

"Oh," I said, suddenly nervous.

"You're going to get more looks than the baked goods," Sara smiled.

Moments later I was surrounded by people crowding the indoor market. Long, wooden tables were drawn to the center of the barn and covered in every type of fruit and vegetable, bread, and fabric I could imagine. All around me packages were being unwrapped with careful hands, exchanged, and inspected.

I heard Odessa's name and saw a young woman approach us. Then she was asking about me, her head bent slightly in concern. Odessa introduced us as I tried to smile, repeating the lies I'd told everyone else.

Moments later she moved on, only to be replaced by an older man and his wife. They asked the same questions, had the same look in their eyes only this time the woman reached out, touched my arm and offered to help me in any way she could.

No one should have to experience what I went through, and no man should have ever taken aim at a defenseless woman.

I thanked her, knowing she was right even if the context was wrong.

"Will you be coming to the barn dance tomorrow night?" she asked, and I nodded, hoping I would be back home tomorrow night and not worrying about a stupid party.

One glance over my shoulder and I knew Louise was watching,

a half-smile on her face that said she enjoyed the attention. A man came up behind her and she spun around, pointed back to me.

I stood still, voices seeming to echo in the large space; hushed, joyful, angry. I felt hot, the buckshot beginning to throb again. It hadn't bothered me much in the past few days.

I felt my face flush and braced myself against one of the tables for support.

"Are you all right?" Odessa asked, coming closer, and I nodded, wondering where my fear had come from.

"She looks pale, Dess," Sara said. "Maybe this was too much for her."

"No," I said, shaking my head, "I'm fine. It's just so many people."

"Just stay by my side," Odessa said, taking my arm again and leading me through the crowd.

Sara didn't wander far but seemed to enjoy Odessa's company and I wondered if there might be a time I could talk to her alone and if she would possibly be willing to help me.

"The men in town are going after those bandits," she said, drawing my attention. I realized how happy she was, how her chances of jeopardizing the life she'd made were pretty close to zero. "Do you think you would recognize any of them if they were caught?"

I touched my forehead, the heat building in my side again and scanned the crowd for Odessa, who was at the next table buying some bread.

"They're probably long gone by now," I said, uncomfortable with her question as I picked up an apple and pretended to examine it. "Can I ask you something?"

She nodded eagerly and I took a slow breath, unsure if I was doing the right thing.

"Would you believe me if I said my story wasn't entirely true?"

She took a small step towards me, anxious for more gossip. "Really?"

I nodded. "I'm not from here, Sara."

She waved her hand, annoyed that my tidbit wasn't exciting. "We know... you're from south of Kalamazoo."

"No," I held her gaze, praying she would believe me. "I came from another place. And another time."

I watched her eyebrows knit together, watched her pretty face go pale as she took a quick step away. "Who are you?"

"I think you know," I said. "And I think you understand what the Whisper Stone can do."

At first, she looked like I'd slapped her, the color draining from her face only to return moments later in an angry rush.

"I'm sure I don't," she said, her voice shaking, and I reached out, touched her hand only to have her draw away quickly.

"You don't understand," I began, desperate now that I had begun. "Andrew's life is in danger."

Her eyes widened as her hand went to her mouth.

"Andrew?" she asked, and I nodded, hoping she would listen when a sudden movement caught my eye.

I felt my mouth go dry, unable to calm the frantic beating of my heart as he approached- his form and figure just as I remembered, the voice I loved above all others asking if everything was all right.

"Dylan?" I just managed, the heartbeat in my temples bleeding into a blackness that stole my sight as I tumbled to the floor at his feet.

CHAPTER
EIGHT

"Justine?" I heard Odessa say as if she were speaking to me underwater and I stirred, tried to open my eyes, and felt arms around me, holding me in place.

"Easy," the voice said. "You hit your head when you fell."

"Fell?" I repeated, light piercing my eyelids and I opened them, the people I'd come to know standing over me. But the one holding me, the one who had just spoken...

"Dylan?" I asked again, his blue eyes coming into focus as I blinked.

"No," he said, his voice making me doubt my senses.

"Who are you?" I asked, feeling like I should know, my fingers going to my forehead where a lump was forming.

"I'm Andrew Karsten, Miss."

"Andrew?" I repeated, the memory of him bleeding to death on the snowy moss returning now.

But inside the barn- in the half- light- with my heart raw and aching for the man I loved...

"You must have thought he was your beau," Sara bent closer, an intensity to her eyes I hadn't seen before.

"Yes," I said, struggling to sit up as a crushing despair washed over me. "I'm so sorry."

"Don't be," Sara continued. "I expect the shock of the last few days has made you mistaken about a great many things."

I looked at her, holding her gaze for a moment.

"Whatever is going on here!" Louise cried from beyond the curious onlookers. The next moment the Cook matriarch appeared, red faced and sweating as she took stock of what had happened.

"Has she fallen?" she turned to her daughter; her hands balled into fists that seemed to be stuck to her hips. "I suspected this was too much and now we are certain to be set back."

Odessa shook her head, a glimmer in her eyes. "You were the one who wanted her to come."

I looked at Louise and allowed Andrew Karsten to help me to my feet.

"I hardly think I would be so foolish," her mother retorted. "But now I see we must get her home."

"No," I said, looking around me for the first time. We were in the middle of the barn, a crowd of people gathered just beyond Odessa. People were shaking their heads, sunbonnets bobbing as the women whispered behind their hands about how long Louise would be able to look after me. "I want to stay."

Louise puffed out her cheeks, let the breath out slowly as she surveyed the audience.

"Well, take her outside for pity's sake," she scolded. "The air may do her some good."

The next minute she was gone, and I turned to the man who had helped me, seeing the differences now in the shape of his face, the scar on his chin and the color of his hair and eyes, which were lighter than Dylan's.

"You sure you're all right, Miss?"

I nodded, and when he smiled my heart did a flip flop. Dead-ringer there.

"I'm fine," I said. "And I'm so pleased to meet you, Mr. Karsten. Sara and I were just talking about you."

He turned to her, a pleased look on his face. "You were?"

"Yes," I said, and Sara tensed, Odessa's eyes cutting between the three of us. "She was telling me about how happy you are, and I told her how lucky she was."

"You did?" he asked, the smile twisting my gut again.

"And I told her she shouldn't take it for granted because it would be a real shame if something bad happened."

The smile vanished, a look of confusion replacing it and I watched Sara press her lips together, clearly struggling.

"I don't understand," he echoed. "Miss,"

I took a deep breath, raised my shoulders as if to say everything was fine again.

"I'm just thinking about my beau. Forgive me. I'm going to step outside and clear my head."

"Justine?" Odessa asked. "Are you sure?"

I nodded, turning my back on the other two while making my way towards the door.

Once outside, I walked away from the barn, the chilly air poking at my face and making my aching joints throb. Taking a few deep breaths, I thought about Cal and where he might be, wondering if I'd made a terrible mistake by confiding in Sara Bennett when I heard a quick step behind me.

Spinning, I raised my chin as she approached, her body rigid as she fought to suppress her anger or fear or whatever else was eating her alive.

"I heard you loud and clear back there and you'd better tell me what the *hell* is going on!"

I scanned the yard for Andrew and Odessa, but they had not followed her outside.

"I came to look after you but it's for one reason and one reason only," Sara said, her finger in my face. "How do you know about the Whisper Stone?"

I stood still for a moment, allowing her to take a breath before I began to speak.

"You told me."

She didn't move at first, her eyes narrowing as if she didn't believe me.

"I've never laid eyes on you before this day."

I reached out to touch her hand and she tensed but did not pull away. "But what about *after* this day?"

"After?" she repeated weakly. "I don't understand,"

"I think you do," I said. "And I think you can help me."

"I can't," she said. "Andrew knows nothing about where I came from. I told him I'd lost my family, that I was all alone and if he finds out,"

"He'll understand."

"He won't believe me," she said, her hands clasped in front of her stomach again. "He'll leave me."

"No. "

"Dylan hasn't made it through, has he?" she said, and I felt my anger rise.

"No."

"And he never will," she came closer, her eyes hard. "Go back to wherever it is you came from. And stay there."

I looked away, despair settling across my shoulders. "There won't be anything to go back to if I don't find the medicine bag."

She stopped, narrowed her eyes again. "Esther told me Odessa used it to tell fortunes. I bet she did something to you as well. That's why you're saying these crazy things,"

"No."

"I can't help you," she said, pausing before turning back towards the barn. "No one can."

I stood helplessly, convinced that I had ruined any chance of finding the totems when I heard voices rising from inside the barn.

Shouting. Commotion. Agitation.

A figure ran out the open door towards me and it took a moment before I realized who it was.

"Odessa?" I cried, and she came to me, grasping my hands, her eyes wild with fear.

"The Cuppy girl has fallen into the river," she said, and I searched my memory, wondering why she would react so strongly to someone I'd never heard of.

"Who is she?" I asked.

"Cal," she whispered, pulling me along as she ran away from the Jennison Barn and towards the forest.

My heart stopped. "What about him?"

"He was with her," she slid to a halt. "They think he fell in, too."

I gripped her arm, thinking of the boy who looked like Adam and couldn't imagine how Odessa would survive without him.

How *I* would survive...

But Calvert Cook didn't drown, he'd lived to a ripe old age after passing Butler's wisdom to his children, who had then passed it on to their children.

I froze, terror numbing my skin as I thought about Cal's ordinary routine, displaced now because of me.

I stood like a stone, horrified that something I'd said or done had caused him to change course, leading him to the river and if the Cuppy girl fell in...

There was no way Cal wouldn't have gone in after her.

"Dess," Andrew's voice jolted me, and I turned to see him standing with Sara, the eyes he shared with Dylan carrying the same haunted expression I'd seen countless times before.

I watched my grandmother nod, watched her gaze wander to the forest before she pulled herself to her full height, her voice like the shot from a rifle.

"Let's go."

CHAPTER
NINE

Cal spent most of the morning with the shaman, had gone with him into the woods to a place called the Whisper Stone - a large rock with strange markings that rose above a bed of reindeer moss.

Butler told him of the great wind piercing like an archer's arrows, carrying people back to their ancestors. He had then pointed to the picture on the rock that told the story and Cal leaned down, touched it with his fingers.

"If you ever need to find me, this is where you must come."

Cal stood straight; his face creased in worry.

"Won't you be at the Rook Cabin?"

Butler's smile softened, his eyes resting on the boy in a way that made Cal feel like he wasn't telling him something.

"I am older than you, and a time will come when I must leave this place and begin my journey into the next."

"Do you mean when you go to Heaven?"

He looked up at Butler and was surprised to see him smiling.

"What do you think it means, Cal?"

At first the boy didn't know how to answer, but then his heart took hold.

"You're good to Ma and me and I don't think anyone like that could go anyplace else."

He felt the shaman's hand on his shoulder again, felt his fingers squeeze.

"But if I'm wrong, and Heaven's full of people like Gran and Preacher then I'd just assume not go."

The shaman's great laugh split the forest. "You are wise, Oshki-nawe, and will be a comfort to your mother."

Once again Cal felt something stir within him, a feeling that the Butler wasn't telling him something.

The harsh call of a crow startled Cal and made him think about his gran, and ma, and the market, the river running through the woods behind the Jennison Barn. He realized he was late.

"I've gotta go!" he cried, "I forgot something."

The shaman's eyes crinkled at the corners, as though he knew who Cal was going to see, the crow circling overhead now, and it made Cal worry.

Uncle Johnny said crows foretold death and Preacher Younts had talked about it at church. He knew he shouldn't be thinking about things like that when Ana was waiting for him, probably mad as a hornet because today they were exchanging the gifts they'd made for each other.

He'd been working away on a cat whittled from a piece of soft birch, in part because Ana was always talking about the kittens that lived in her barn and he knew it would make her happy to know he'd remembered that.

He wondered what gift she would give him, wondered if they would mark only the passing of this day or the beginning of something more as he ran through the forest, the cry of the crow joining him in the trees.

Ducking under a branch, he found the river again and began to follow its path north until he came to a place that widened, a flat clearing of tall cedar that cast shadows on the ground.

"Ana!" he called, his voice carrying above the rushing water, watching as she moved from behind a tree.

She stood still, her arms at her side, as lovely as anything he had ever seen in a red gingham dress, her thick, golden hair hanging in two braids and tied at the ends with ribbons of the same color.

Her cheeks were pink, her lips pursed, and he knew she had been waiting a long time and felt a knot of regret tighten in his stomach.

"Calvert Cook," she scolded, her brown eyes narrowing when she saw him. "I've been standing here for almost half an hour."

He looked down, ashamed to have kept her waiting, and pulled the wooden cat out of his pocket.

"I brought you this," he said, extending his hand and he watched Ana's eyes widen, then soften, and knew she was pleased. "And I'm sorry I'm late. I had to,"

"Run off with the shaman?" she interrupted, an annoyed lilt to her voice.

"Yes," he said, not wanting to hide anything from her. "I was."

He watched her foot tap against the hard earth, watched her fingers twiddle against her hip. "Ma says he talks to animals and dead folks, says he casts spells to make the crops fail."

Cal felt his stomach knot up again. "That's not true."

"And Pa says it's not fitting for him to spend time with your ma when Preacher intends to court her." She paused. "There's talk he might propose at the barn dance."

Cal stiffened, ready to endure a thousand beatings if it meant the preacher would leave his ma alone.

"Does it bother you, Cal?" she asked, looking at him closely.

"Ana,"

"I mean," she swallowed, one hand coming up to run the

length of the braid that laid over her right shoulder. "Wouldn't it be nice to have a pa?"

"I don't know."

"You don't know?" she echoed; shaking her head.

Cal wanted to shout that she was right and that he did want a pa and that the shaman was the closest he'd ever come to that.

"What do you think?" he asked.

She cocked her head sideways.

"What does it matter what I think? Ma says,"

"I didn't ask what your ma thought, Ana. I wanna know what *you* think."

He watched as a smile crept slowly across her face. "You do?"

He nodded.

He watched her pull her bottom lip between her teeth, watched her forehead pucker.

"Well, I suppose he helps an awful lot with the farm since Johnny,"

She stopped short, a slight flush in her cheeks and Cal knew she didn't want to talk about what was wrong with Johnny, knew that no one wanted to talk about it.

He stood unsure what to say.

"Don't worry about it, Cal," she said. "Soon enough you'll have the farm, and we'll work it together."

He glanced at her sharply, unsure he'd heard her right.

"I mean," she stammered, suddenly red in the face. "Here's what I made for you."

She held out her hand and Cal leaned closer, saw a lover's knot woven from some sort of soft reed that grew along the river and threaded with a blue ribbon.

He drew in his breath, unable to believe she had given him something so wonderful that he could hide in his pocket and touch from time to time.

"There," she said, laying her palm flat and Cal reached down, his hand sliding over hers and he felt a lump rise in his throat, felt the wind come from behind, bringing the scent of her hair and the soap she'd washed it with.

The next moment he was leaning towards her, the distance between them sliding away like the long shadows at evening as his lips brushed hers.

A little gasp bubbled up from deep within her throat and Cal hoped it was because she was happy, because he was happy, never realizing until that moment how quickly life could change.

The next moment she was pulling away and skipping in a circle.

"I've been wanting a kiss for a good long while, Calvert Cook!"

He smiled, a sigh of relief escaping. "Really?"

"Ever since you hit that awful LeRoy Burks square in the face when he called your ma a name."

"Really?" he asked again, his memory resting on that day last spring after Butler had helped plant the garden.

He could see LeRoy at recess, his voice rising above the others as he said things that couldn't be true, things he saw while walking by their farm and it made Cal so mad, he couldn't see straight.

He remembered knocking LeRoy off his feet, remembered his fists pummeling his freckled face until Ms. Cunningham pulled them apart. He'd stood up, swiping at his bloody lip as Ana stood off to the side, watching him like she was right now.

"If you catch me, you can kiss me again."

"Really?" he asked, unable to believe he could feel this kind of happiness.

She burst out laughing. "Is that all you can say?"

He shook his head, took off after her as she dashed behind another tree, her skirt catching the wind as the crow circled overhead. Cal caught sight of it, his heart too light to care as he took hold of Ana's arm. One spin and she was next to him again, her lips pressing into his but this time she brought her hand to his cheek, her fingers just tangling in his hair, and he could hardly feel his arms or legs anymore.

Then she was gone again, clearly enjoying this game and Cal reached for her only to have her dart off in another direction, the water joining their laughter.

She was close to the bank now and Cal drew up sharply, a memory resurfacing.

They had gone to the Big Lake for a church picnic, but Ana had stayed away from the water and sat on the beach, her head on top of her knees as Cal left the others to sit beside her.

"Don't you want to go in the lake?" he asked.

She shook her head. "Can't swim."

"Why not?" he asked, trying not to make her feel bad and she had looked up at him with those big eyes, her nose and cheeks red.

"Pa never had time to teach me."

Cal remembered touching his shoulder to hers, promising her he would do it but that day never came and now she was leaning backwards, the soft bank crumbling beneath her as she tumbled into the water.

"Ana!" Cal cried, sprinting over to where she had vanished.

Her head was just there, bobbing like a cork at the end of a fishing pole while the current pulled her towards the middle where the water was swift.

Cal knew that many trees had fallen across the river, knew their branches reached like gnarled fingers beneath the water, pulling people under and it wouldn't matter if Ana had known how to swim.

She would drown.

"Cal," she gasped, her hands reaching towards him, and he fell to his knees, put his arm out and she grasped his wrist, her hold fierce, her eyes on fire as the current tugged at her wet dress. "Don't let go."

He tightened his grip, knowing he would die before he did that and wished for Butler's medicine to find him here, on the riverbank.

The crow's cry startled him, rising high above the rush of water and he felt his heart freeze, felt his body sliding forward and knew his only choice was to be pulled into the water beside Ana.

He fell forward and felt the cold crush pummel him, fingers from long-drowned trees grabbing his ankle, holding him still as Ana's hand was ripped from his.

"Ana!" he cried again, stuck in place as the current caught hold, carrying her downstream and beneath the water.

Cal gasped, felt water fill his lungs and thought of his ma, fearing he wouldn't be there to comfort her like the shaman had said.

Instead, Butler would have to help her.

"Ana!" he cried again, thinking of where she might be, wondering if he could keep fighting.

If he even wanted to.

The water was pulling him down, the branch catching one moment, releasing him the next. He tumbled into the current, his arms and legs useless as he hit a rock, his head exploding in pain.

The next moment he was shooting down the river, the forest whizzing by in a green blur while darkness settled around the edge of his vision.

He watched the trees, watched the sunlight filter between the shadows of the cedar glen and heard the crow, knowing now that Uncle Johnny and the preacher had been right.

Cal looked to the forest again, felt exhaustion cup his skull and saw a man kneeling near the shore, his back to him.

"Help," he gasped, his arms flailing above his head and the man stood up quickly and turned.

You have an angel- his ma used to say when tucking him into bed, and Cal believed this man was just that as he ran towards the riverbank.

"Andrew!" he gasped, praying his friend could help when another rock hit him between the shoulder blades, knocking the breath from him.

Cal watched as he rushed to the edge, reaching out towards him as the water closed over his head and swallowed him whole.

CHAPTER

TEN

I ran through the autumn woods towards the river, wishing for the speed Butler had yet to give me, Odessa's long braid flying behind her as I fought to keep up.

People had gathered on the banks, watching as the water rushed by in a frothy foam.

I pulled up short, looked to Andrew and Sara, wondering if she had told him anything.

Knowing she hadn't.

"How do they know this is where she fell in?" I panted, my heart beating in my ears, my feet on fire.

"Rachel Cuppy went looking when she didn't come home for chores," Andrew explained. "She knew Ana loved this place and she found a lover's knot she'd made for Cal on the bank where the side of it had caved in."

Sara shook her head, her hands unconsciously covering her stomach again.

"Odessa," I turned to her. "Where was Cal going today?"

She looked again to the forest behind her, her movements agitated.

"He was going to meet us after he saw Ana. He made a gift for her, too," she paused, her brow furrowing as she tried to remember. "A little cat he'd been whittling away at," she stopped, put a trembling hand over her face. "I knew that water was running fast after the storms we've had. I should have told him to stay away, should have made him come with me."

I touched her shoulder. "Do you think he went in after her?"

She drew a breath, unable to speak but I knew what her silence meant.

"The river splits in two up ahead," Andrew said, and I turned, looked into his eyes and felt a rush of relief that stole my breath. "It's likely the water is swifter in the south branch and will take them that way."

I nodded, his words reminding me of Dylan and realized their similarities went far beyond the physical.

Turning, I saw Odessa ahead of us, her cries mixing with our own as she called out for her boy.

I struggled to keep up, slowing my pace to match my burning feet, my eyes searching for Cal's dark head amongst the clutter of branches that gave the river its wild appearance.

Glancing behind again, I saw Andrew take Sara's hand and felt a wave of longing so strong it almost sent me to my knees.

Make the path, Muffet...

Dad's words as I lay asleep in Cabin Ten came back to me, and I turned, expecting to see him lingering in some corner of the yellow wood. I thought of the necklace I now wore, once buried beneath the hickory trees, and touched the silver circle.

White noise filled my ears, Odessa's skirt bleeding into the trees until it became the weathered stone of the Presque Isle Lighthouse.

Someone was walking in front of me, a boy holding a lantern high above his head- a boy who looked like Cal but was somehow different.

I picked up my skirts, took off at a dead run.

"Adam!" I cried, reaching out to touch him from behind and he stopped, turned slowly.

I fell to my knees, took him into my arms and felt him bury his head against my shoulder.

YOU HAVE TO FIND IT

I pulled back, looked into his eyes and knew it took everything he had to come to me here. "I'm trying, but the medicine bag is still missing and I don't want to screw everything up-"

NOT THAT

I froze, afraid of what he might say next.

ESTHER MADE A HOME FOR THE STARS

"What?" I asked. "How do I find them?"

THEY LIVE WHERE HENRY YOUNTS DIED

"Where he died?" I repeated, and my brother stepped away, raised the lantern high again and I knew that he was leaving me. "You mean on the island in the middle of the marsh?"

BEFORE THAT

I looked at my brother, wishing he could stay as he vanished into the trees and I stood still, my feet burning again as Sara's voice rang in my ear.

"She's bleeding!"

I blinked, felt the world materialize before me and put a shaking hand to my mouth. A metallic taste had gathered there and I glanced down, saw that my fingers were stained red.

"Justine," Andrew said, bending down so he could get a better look at my face. "Are you all right?"

"I'm fine," I lied, turning away in the slightest, still off balance from the vision. "I get nosebleeds."

"Here," Andrew said while handing me a handkerchief, his voice carrying me back to all the times Dylan had comforted me. And beyond that, to the safety I'd felt in Troy's arms on the deck of the Pink Pony.

"Thank you," I said quickly as I wiped at my face, my head

spinning as I thought about what the blood coupled with my brother's appearance might mean.

ADAM?

I said the word cautiously, hoping he would answer and was greeted with silence.

I felt my heartbeat in my ears, the taste of metal on my tongue as Sara bent to look at me, a strange dawning in her eyes.

"You seem like you're a million miles away," she said.

I looked at her, remembering my brother's words about the stars when a strangled cry came from down the riverbank. Odessa was on her knees beside the water holding something in her hand.

At once I took off running, my fear choking me as I went to my knees beside her.

"What?" I asked, taking her hand and prying it open. "What is it?"

"It's the cat he made for her," she said, her voice spilling into a sob.

I looked at the object and felt my stomach turn over.

"It doesn't mean anything," I said, trying to comfort her. "It could have fallen out of Ana's hand. Or Cal's- before he went in after her."

"No," she said, shaking her head. "He's in the water."

"How do you know that?"

"I feel it," she said, her eyes sliding closed. "*He* feels it..."

Something moved in my peripheral vision.

Instinct told me that I would need my feet beneath me when this person came into view, and so I stood, watching as he emerged from the forest like the mist at dawn, his strides quickening as he saw the woman beside me.

"Dess," he said, going to her and I stood frozen in place. Barely breathing, my gaze dropped from his face to his faded cotton shirt and canvas pants before resting on a rawhide pouch hanging from his belt.

"Butler," Odessa said, her voice catching, and I felt my knees begin to shake, unable to move or speak or even breathe as the shaman's dark eyes found mine.

CHAPTER
ELEVEN

C al felt something cold beneath his cheek, the wet leaves that lined the river sticking to his skin and wondered where he was. He remembered Ana dancing on the side of the bank, remembered the lover's knot she had made for him and then the rock hitting him in the head, making everything dark and heavy.

There had been a person running between the trees, a person he thought was Andrew.

"Can you hear me?" a voice asked.

Cal groaned, felt a pair of hands touching his shoulders and wondered if his ma was looking for him and if Uncle Johnny would be angry because he hadn't helped in the fields.

"Can you move?"

He swallowed, felt a throbbing in the back of his head where the rock had hit him and opened his eyes.

Sunlight sifted between the trees, and he had no idea where he was or how he had gotten out of the river's deadly grasp. A man was leaning over him, the man he'd thought was Andrew but now...

"Can you talk to me?"

Cal blinked, tried to swallow again and found that his throat was dry, the throbbing in his head nearly drowning out the man's voice and still something told him not to be afraid.

"I," he began, searching in his memory for what had happened. "I fell in."

"I know," the man said, his blue eyes flecked with concern. "I pulled you out."

There was something hanging from the man's neck, a circle with a cross that looked like the one Justine wore around her neck.

His mind clamped down on her.

"She has one of those," he managed, his finger pointing to it.

"What?" the man asked. "Who does?"

Cal tried to remember, his mind spinning to the dark trees and the crow's call and the ribbons in Ana's hair.

He saw the necklace- circle cut into four parts and remembered something Butler had told him last spring, something about how everything became clear if you looked with new eyes

"Justine," he whispered as the man's hands slid behind his shoulders, easing him against the trunk of an oak tree. "She was dancing."

"Dancing?" the stranger repeated. "Where?"

Cal thought of the necklace again.

"Beside the river. I went in after her."

He felt something in the man shift.

"You did," he said, and something in his voice reminded Cal of how he'd felt when Ana's hand had been ripped from his. "Where is she now?"

He tried to remember the last time he'd seen her.

It was that morning as she was stuffing her feet into his ma's old shoes. They had laughed together about Johnny burning her clothes and she told him she would gladly add these to the fire.

"She was in the field," he said, thinking again of the moment he first found her. "There was blood on her shirt."

He felt the man's fingers grip and release. "*Where is she now?*"

Cal tried to remember if she was dancing with Ana or disappearing into the woods as the bandits shot at her from shore. "I don't know," he whispered, his head throbbing. "I don't,"

"Try to remember," the man cut him off.

"I can't," Cal said, the heaviness clamping down hard and he wondered if he would be in trouble for leaving the farm, for meeting Ana, for kissing her. "It hurts."

He thought about her yellow braids and felt the breeze steal his breath.

"What's your name?" the man asked, his voice desperate and Cal wanted to tell him, wanted to wander to the door of the Rook Cabin again and make the sound of the whippoorwill.

"Cal!" a voice rose above the water and the man stood quickly.

Heavy footfalls in the underbrush- large boots crushing leaves.

He felt the throbbing in his head again, tried to look for the man but he was gone.

At once Preacher Younts appeared from the surrounding forest and knelt beside him, touching his shoulder as the man with the blue eyes had done only moments before.

"Where is he?" Cal asked, his voice barely a whisper and the preacher bent closer.

"Who?" he asked, his face twisting with what could have been mistaken for relief.

"He pulled me out," he whispered. "He was right beside me."

"There's no one here," Preacher said.

"Yes," the boy insisted. "*I saw him.*"

"No," he cut him off. "You're alone."

"Ana,"he said, his heart hanging on his answer.

"She'll be found."

"But_"

The sound of the crow came again, carried far above their heads as the preacher looked to the treetops.

"The bird," the boy managed, blackness stealing his vision

again. "I know what it means. I heard it right before I saw Ana and-
"

"Hush," Henry Younts repeated, looking up one last time before gathering the boy in his arms. "Let's get you back to your ma."

～

I STOOD FROZEN as Butler approached, a million thoughts flying through my mind, unable to believe I was sharing this moment on the riverbank with him.

I opened my mouth, watched his dark eyes move to Odessa.

Sara and Andrew approached, and I saw them nod as they passed, telling us they would continue looking further downstream.

The next moment Odessa was in his arms, and he pulled her close, his hands tightening on her back and I stood still, wondering if I should look away.

"Dess," he said once he'd seen her face. "What happened?"

"Cal," she whispered, unable to say the rest and I stood as straight as I could, my head just reaching the shaman's shoulder.

"He fell in the river," I managed, my voice faltering, my eyes dropping to the medicine bag again. I remembered the first time I'd seen it, hidden inside of my old birthday present. I remembered taking it from the box, holding it in my hands as I uncinched the rawhide and spread the totems on Iris' kitchen table.

"Who is this?" Butler asked, stepping away from her and I felt naked under his gaze, as though he could see through the folds of time to who I really was.

"This is Justine," Odessa spoke. "She's the one I've been nursing."

"Yes," Butler said, as though he'd already known, and I wondered if Odessa told him in a stolen moment.

"We're waiting on her beau to come for her," she said. "Although I don't know what I'll do without her."

I felt my heart warm as Butler stood still, his face unreadable.

"Are you sure he fell in?"

"I found this," she opened her hand, showed him the wooden cat. "They must be nearby."

"He is a strong swimmer," the shaman said while scanning the river.

"It won't matter," Odessa said, her fingers on her mouth, her lower lip trembling. "He'll be swept away."

Butler drew her to him again, his fingers trailing down the long braid that hung past the middle of her back and I glanced down, knowing Odessa must be out of her mind with worry or she would never allow me to witness such intimacy.

"He is not gone, Little One," Butler whispered. "I would feel it."

She looked up and he touched her cheek, one finger lingering on her jaw.

Then they were moving off ahead of me, down the river towards where Sara and Andrew had gone before and I kept a few paces behind, the bloody handkerchief still in my hand as I called for Cal.

It wasn't long before Odessa glanced back at me.

I held her gaze, wondering what she wanted when she turned back to Butler.

The next moment he was speaking low in her ear, and I allowed them to move farther away, hoping some distance would allow them to let down their guard.

The time has come...

I heard his voice as though he were standing beside me.

Do you have all of them?

I stopped walking, let them drift further away.

Yes

Will they help me find my son?

A long pause.

The medicine is just awakening. We must wait and see what it will do.

I watched Butler touch his belt and knew he was untying the medicine bag, placing it in my grandmother's hand moments later.

Keep it safe.

I felt my limbs go heavy, felt the power that had been given to my family settle across my shoulders like a leaden weight and knew nothing could be undone now.

I called for Cal again, my voice weakened in the wind and wondered if Louise had made her way to the river and if she and Johnny were looking for him. I walked, the people I had risked everything to find just ahead and wondered what I should do.

Make the path, Muffet...

I saw Dad in his silver canoe, the sun in his hair as the willow just brushed the water. Then he was being pushed away on the wind, towards the day when my life changed forever.

I picked up my pace, their voices dying as I came up behind them.

The sky was darkening, and it made me wonder how long we had been gone and why dusk would come so soon as a flicker of light danced between the long shadows cast by the forest.

It leapt just above the ground, moving between the trees and at once I heard a sharp cry in the distance, tempered by the rushing water.

"They've found something," Odessa said, her words tumbling on top of each other, and I felt the earth stop spinning, felt my fear take form and if Cal had been found dead in the water...

I shut the thought out, trudged on as the light came closer, dancing within the glass box that imprisoned it.

Another appeared further down the bank, and then another until the edge of the river seemed to glow like a string of fireflies.

"If a child becomes lost the lanterns will lead them home," Odessa stood beside me now, her gaze following the line that seemed to glow like a lighted path through the forest.

"They will?"

My grandmother nodded. "They will burn all night long."

I took a breath, thought back to the fairy tales of my childhood and felt like I'd wandered into a dream.

"Do the children find their way home?"

She turned to me, her face set like stone.

"Once."

I stood watching them, wondering if they would say more when a voice broke free from the forest.

"Odessa!"

I started, turned towards the sound.

"Odessa!" the voice called again. "We've found him! Pa's found him!"

I felt my body loosen in relief as a lantern approached, carried quickly by a person who had just emerged from the fading light.

I gasped, unable to stop myself, a longing so deep it stole my breath as Jamie Stoddard came to a sudden stop in front of me.

CHAPTER
TWELVE

I felt my knees go weak as I took in his brown hair, always out of place, and the amber eyes, which widened when they saw me and in the far reaches of my mind, I wanted him to know me.

I saw him leaning on an upended bucksaw, saw him in the dashboard light of his truck- the old man who had come to say goodbye while I lay in the hospital, and realized I'd missed him every day since.

"Odessa," he repeated, his gaze sweeping from me to her, and then Butler. "Pa has Cal. He took him back to our place and sent for Doc."

I watched the woman before me fall to her knees, watched her reach for Jamie's hand and hold it against her face.

We were silent, standing around her in a strange, semi-circle as she choked on her words.

"He's-" she stopped, and Butler came closer, placed a hand on her shoulder. "He's alive, then?"

Jamie nodded, his eyes cutting to me in the lantern light.

"He hit his head and is saying some things that don't make sense."

"I need to get to him," Odessa whispered, and Jamie pulled back, his eyes on me again.

"Who's this?" he asked, and for a blissful moment I imagined him slinging his arm around my shoulder while we talked about which canoes needed to be cleaned out at Three Fires.

"My name is Justine," I just managed, the grief of losing him stronger now that we were together. "The Cooks are taking care of me."

"Yes," he nodded, the crooked smile I remembered breaking through. "Pa told me about you."

"He did?' I asked, feeling like the earth was going soft beneath my feet.

"He'll be glad to know you're up and about."

"He will?" I asked, unable to hide my disbelief.

"We've been remembering you in our prayers," Jamie said. "Pa doesn't take kindly to men who shoot at women."

I wanted to laugh, wanted to tell him it was his father's fault I had a load of buckshot in my side, but bit my lip instead.

"Thank you," Butler spoke up, uncertain of his place. "For coming to find us."

Jamie looked at the shaman, nodded briefly.

"We need to get to the cabin. He's been calling for both of you."

"Both of us?" Odessa asked, rising to her feet.

"You and Justine," Jamie said. "Pa sent me to fetch you."

I watched a look pass between my grandmother and the shaman as she got to her feet.

"Of course."

I took me a moment to match their pace as we trekked through the darkening wood. I found myself staring at the back of Jamie's head, watching the slide of his shoulders as he forged a path in front of us and made my way to his side, desperate for our familiar rapport in a place where no one knew me.

"Something wrong with your shoes?" he asked while looking at me out of the corner of his eye.

I started, then realized I'd been limping along, my feet a ball of fire. "Odessa gave them to me. Seems these fit her before Cal was born."

"Don't you have your own?"

I shook my head, tried to hide my smile. "Johnny burned them."

A pause. "He did?"

"Yes," I said. "All my clothes, actually, but the shoes seem to be the hardest to replace."

Jamie shook his head, smiled again.

"Well, Johnson Cook has done some fool things, but this beats all."

I gave an awkward laugh, unsure how to talk to treat him like a stranger.

"My mother was about your size. Maybe I can get Pa to part with a pair."

I frowned, disturbed by the thought of cramming my feet into Henry Younts' dead wife's shoes.

"You don't like that idea?" he asked.

"No," I said quickly, not wanting to offend him. "I don't want to impose... if they belonged to your mother,"

"It's all right," he said. "High time Pa let them go."

I looked at him out of the corner of my eye.

"Has she been gone long?"

He nodded. "One of the horses at the Ebersole Farm threw her when I was ten."

"I'm sorry," I managed, not able to look at him.

"It was a long time ago."

"Jamie," I said before I could help it and he turned, looked at me for a beat before answering.

"My name is Jonas, Miss."

"Of course," I said quickly. "I don't know why I said that."

"Well, you've been through a lot."

I nodded, upset with myself as the lightened window of a cabin appeared between the trees. Odessa broke into a run, swatting branches out of her way as she pushed through the forest and Butler took a step to follow, then stopped.

"If it was up to me, you'd see the boy," Jamie paused. "But Pa's mind is set."

Butler nodded.

"Stay close. She'll need you."

He nodded again, crossed his arms against his chest and sat down at the base of a large oak tree, as content in darkness as he had been in daylight.

I hesitated, watching him for a moment before Jamie motioned for me to enter.

Once inside, I immediately felt my skin begin to prickle and scanned the room for Henry Younts. He was standing against the far wall, Cal on a cot that had been drawn close to the fire as Odessa knelt in front of him.

"Calvert," she whispered as she took hold of his hand. "Why would you do such a fool thing?"

I went to her side, saw that the boy looked feverish and put a hand to his forehead, an image of my brother flashing before my eyes.

ADAM

I said his name again, waiting for the answer that had only come in my dreams.

Cal turned on the bed, his hands twisting the blanket Henry Younts had placed over him, his dark hair plastered to his forehead.

"Cal," I said, my voice low. "Can you hear us?"

Henry Younts shuffled behind me, his large frame casting a shadow across the floor, and I tightened my shoulders, tried not to shrink away.

"Doc was here," he said. "Left some powder for his pain on the table."

Odessa nodded.

"Said he'll be back in the morning and not to move him tonight."

"Yes."

"It's a good thing I found him when I did," he continued. "I don't think he would have lasted much longer in that water."

Odessa turned, tears shining in her eyes as she reached out a hand to him. The color seemed to creep up his face as he took it, his large fingers engulfing hers.

"How did you find him? The current was so fast, I felt sure,"

"Wasn't in the water," Henry Younts interrupted. "He'd gotten out somehow and was lying on the bank."

"Gotten out?" Odessa echoed, fine lines of worry etching her face. "How in the world was he able to do that?"

"Now, Dess," he bent towards her. "It's not our place to question the ways of the Lord. If He saw fit to save your boy, our only job is to be grateful for it."

My grandmother swallowed, his words seeming to comfort her, and I thought of Butler sitting beneath the oak tree, watching the lightened windows of the cabin he was not allowed to enter.

"And what of Ana Cuppy?" she asked.

I felt the room harden around the edges, the soft light of the kerosene lamp seeming to cast shadows and remembered the rushing water, remembered how cold it was and thought of the lanterns burning on the riverbank.

The preacher shook his head, mumbled something about the search continuing through the night when Cal began to stir.

"Cal," his mother said, moving close again. "Can you hear me?"

The boy moaned, his eyes fluttering open, then widening as he took in the sight of us standing around him.

"Ana?" he asked, and Odessa glanced back at me as she pushed his hair off his forehead, her face pinched.

"We'll find her," his mother said. "The lanterns have been lit."

"The lanterns," the boy repeated, and I wondered how many times they had burned through the night and what had become of the child who found his way home.

"How did you get out?" Odessa asked, her hands tightening around her son's. "Preacher said he found you on the bank."

I watched Cal stir again, twisting beneath the blanket as his eyes found me.

"He pulled me out."

I turned toward Henry Younts and his face hardened.

"That's not true, boy. You was on the bank when I found you."

"Not you," Cal whispered. "It was someone else."

"Who was it, son?" Odessa asked.

He pointed to me. "Her necklace,"

I touched the spot where it lay hidden beneath the buttons of my dress.

"What?" I asked.

Cal looked at me, his face flushed, his eyes on fire.

"He had one just like it."

CHAPTER

THIRTEEN

I felt my heart seize up, felt my arms and legs and fingers and toes go numb with an ecstasy I didn't know I could experience.

"Justine," Odessa began, turning to me. "What is he talking about?"

"Cal," I whispered, barely able to form the word as my fingers sought the buttons on my dress. Falling on my knees, I yanked the necklace free and held it in front of him. "Are you saying he had this?"

He looked at the necklace, then at me, and nodded again.

"Are you sure?" I whispered, my fingers shaking so badly I could barely hold it.

"Yes," he said, and I felt the room spin.

"What is it?" Odessa asked, her hand on my shoulder.

I couldn't answer, could only grip the blanket on Cal's bed while images of the man I loved filled my mind. I saw him leaning down to look at me through Holly's car window, felt his body press against me as we lingered in the bed we shared.

I saw his silhouette, awash in silver as we watched *Casablanca* on our couch, saw him trace a sentence in a textbook as he studied at the kitchen table, felt his hand in mine as we stood on the Whisper Stone, waiting for the great wind to carry us away.

"He knew about you," Cal whispered, and I lifted my head, my life hanging on his every word. "He asked where you were."

I took his hand, squeezed so hard I thought his bones might break.

"Did you tell him?"

He shook his head, and I felt the cold fingers of fear brush my skin.

"Preacher started calling for me and," he paused, took a breath. "He ran away."

"Ran away?" I asked, ice water in my veins. "Where did he go?"

"I don't know."

"What do you mean *you don't know?*"

Cal shook his head, his forehead furrowed. "I couldn't see him and then Preacher was there and,"

"What did he look like?"

"Justine," Odessa interrupted. "I don't think,"

"What did he look like?" I cried, still gripping Cal as Henry Younts moved from behind, one hand going to my shoulder, and I jolted at his touch, shrugged him off as though his fingers were made of fire.

"I thought he was Andrew at first,"

I stood up.

"It's Dylan."

Odessa's eyes widened.

"But how did he get here? Johnny just sent the letter off yesterday."

"Maybe he heard about the bandits," Jamie offered, and I felt my heart leap and twirl like the autumn leaves that had crossed our path that morning.

Dylan was here.

And he was looking for me.

Which meant I needed to get the hell out of this cabin.

"Where did you find Cal?" I turned to Henry Younts, still unable to meet his eyes.

I heard him sigh before answering, "If you think I'm takin' you back there tonight you are sorely mistaken."

I took a step towards him, lifted my chin.

"Then I'll go without you."

Henry Younts smiled, his eyes hard.

"I'd like to see you try."

Jamie stirred in the corner, clearly uncomfortable with the idea.

"Pa,"

"Now, Henry," Odessa said, her tone soft and I looked over, surprised to see her calm. "What harm would it do to help her? This man is her beau, and he must be very worried."

"Dess,"

"There's no telling how far he may wander."

"Now,"

"If you ask me, you are just the man to lead her."

Henry Younts scratched the back of his head.

"Please," she continued. "It would set my mind at rest."

He seemed shaken. "What about the boy?"

Odessa's eyes went to Cal, who had fallen asleep again. "I'll give him the powder Doc left. We'll take him home in the morning."

I watched the color climb Henry Younts' neck and imagined he must be thinking about Odessa spending the night under his roof.

"Jonas can go with you," she continued. "And then you can continue the search for Ana."

"But,"

"There's no use staying here now that Cal is safe."

"Dess," he said again, almost helpless and I watched my grandmother move towards the man I feared, watched her touch his forearm lightly with the tips of her fingers.

"It's your duty, Henry."

"My duty," he repeated, almost dazed and I watched Odessa's hold tighten against his skin and remembered the moment I laid hands on Chelsea and Brad, remembered Adam touching Ethan as he sat on the barstool at Huffs.

"Yes," she said. "Now go. I'll draw the latchstring after you leave."

"All right," he said, his eyes shifting to me in a way that said he was doing it only for Odessa. "I'll take her to the spot, but I'll be no help after that."

"You'll see her home if nothing comes of it," Odessa said, her voice firm. "And if you see Ma and Johnny, tell them I will see them in the morning."

I watched Henry Younts go still, watched him glance down at the place where Odessa had placed her hand.

"Come on, then," he ordered, shaking his head in the slightest while motioning for his son to follow.

"Thank you," I said, uttering the words I never thought I would to the man I never imagined could help me.

"Be careful, Justine," I heard my grandmother say.

Something in her tone made me look back.

"I will," I answered, unable to say more, remembering what Butler had said about the medicine only just beginning to awaken.

The next moment we were outside, the moon rising above the pines, and I lifted my skirt, my feet throbbing as the shoes bit into my skin. One glance to my left and I saw the oak tree Butler had been sitting against, empty now against the wash of the moon.

I pushed my way forward, and Henry Younts grumbled behind me, his breath labored as we hurried towards the river.

"You think you know the way, do you?" he asked from behind.

I pretended I hadn't heard as I ducked beneath branches, the glittering water of the river just ahead.

"Slow down," the preacher ordered. "I don't intend to lose you in the woods."

I opened my mouth to speak and found I couldn't, found that even as I moved, every fiber of my being screamed to run away from him.

But I needed him, and no way in hell was I blowing my chance to find Dylan because I wanted to murder the man standing behind me.

Then he was beside me, his hand on my arm to slow me and I felt my skin wither beneath his touch.

"He was upstream."

I gritted my teeth, muttered under my breath as his hand tightened.

"You stay behind me, you hear?"

I thought about Odessa wandering the dark woods in search of Butler as my mother cried through the night. I thought about Adam, crouching between this monster and the man I loved, thought about Dylan lying in the woods, unconscious and bleeding from a gash carved into his arm as Troy lay trapped beneath the trunk of a massive pine tree.

And my father... murdered by the same hand that held me now.

"Let me go."

I heard Henry Younts laugh as he turned to look at his son.

"She thinks I'm gonna hurt her," he said. "But truth be told, I ain't done nothing but pray over you and for that you should be grateful."

Jamie stepped closer, fear in his eyes and I knew he'd seen his father's temper turn in the past, knew he'd been living with it since his ma had died.

"I aim to guide you, is all."

I closed my eyes, breathed deeply through my nose, and felt the rage that had always triggered my strength begin to seep through my skin, making it prickle.

"Pa," Jamie said, the one word carrying a thousand others behind it. I felt heat rise in my face, a buzzing noise I recognized drowning out his words as I tightened my muscles. Planting my stance, I made a fist, breaking the hold so quickly Henry Younts stumbled backwards.

His balance lost, he tumbled sideways and stood there, half bent against the trunk of a pine tree, his eyes narrowing in the lantern light.

I looked at him, the top of my head just reaching his chest, and clenched my jaw.

I wanted to hurt him, wanted to take my fists and drive them into his face over and over, wanted to take the gun he had strapped to his belt and blow him away.

But I needed to find Dylan, or nothing I'd done so far would be worth a damn.

"Seems she's a mite stronger than she let on," Henry Younts said. "Funny how those things happen when that shaman comes around."

I felt my heart speed up, afraid of what he might know.

"It's just the tonic Doc gave her," Jamie answered. "Nothing more."

"Mayhap," he said. "But you stay clear of him, Miss, or your soul may pay the price."

I raised my eyes, the wind gathering us in a cool embrace.

"It's not my soul you should be worried about."

He went still, and I felt my anger ebb, the fear of losing Dylan replacing it.

"We need to keep moving," I said, and Henry Younts held my gaze before turning back to the darkness.

"Follow me."

FOURTEEN

C al felt himself drifting in and out of consciousness as voices rose from somewhere around the edge of his damp and cloudy mind.

His head hurt from where he had hit the rock, his thoughts muddled as he remembered Ana, wondering if she had been found, thinking of the man with the blue eyes again.

The man who loved Justine.

"Ma," he whispered, able to pick out her voice from the other one.

He waited, felt someone draw close to the strange bed he was lying on and opened his eyes.

She was there, her brown eyes soft as she bent over him.

And then another face, one that made his heart soar.

"Nibwaakaa," he whispered, the shaman's dark eyes swimming before him as he tried to sit up in bed. At once the pain rose to clutch his skull, making his teeth chatter.

"Rest," the shaman said, one hand on his forehead. "We are grateful you are safe."

"Where is everyone?" he asked. "Jonas, Justine..."

"They went to look for the man you saw."

"Ana," he whispered again, visions of her blond braids floating in the cold water haunting him.

He felt his ma take his hand, felt her lips press to his skin. "Preacher is leading the others in a search that will last through the night."

He shook his head, worried they wouldn't find her, wanting to go join the search even as his heart longed to stay where the three of them could be together.

As if he knew his thoughts, the shaman bent closer.

"Your mother and I will stay with you tonight and I will give you some tonic from the willow tree we gathered. Do you remember?"

Cal smiled. He liked the idea of his ma and Butler taking care of him- feeling safe even as his heart settled in uncertainty.

"You must know something, Cal," his mother said, soft yet firm. "When Butler spoke of not having to worry anymore about Gran or Johnny or even Preacher Younts, he spoke the truth."

Cal nodded.

He'd never doubted the shaman's word.

"But you can't tell anyone," his mother said, and he saw the bottle of tonic she had for him and opened his mouth, felt her pour a few drops of the bitter liquid on his tongue. "Or they might take the medicine bag away."

Cal scrunched up his nose, disgusted by the taste as their voices drifted away again, broken only when he heard the shaman.

He was standing beside his bed, an eagle feather in his hand as he ran it down the side of Cal's face and across the back of his head. He had shown him how to do the healing ceremony once before, when he had taken out his drum at the Rook Cabin.

Cal remembered the sound, remembered how it made him feel like he was in another place and Butler had said that was good, that he had something inside of him that others did not.

He watched his ma come closer, watched her pull a small table over to the side of the bed, the medicine bag in her hand.

Uncinching the rawhide strap that held it closed, she took each totem out and arranged them in a circle with the snakeskin in the center.

"This will help you, Oshkinawe," Butler said, his feather sweeping over the top of the totems as he began to say words Cal did not understand.

He smelled something, knew Butler was burning sage and cedar as he had before and breathed in the sweet smell. And then the feeling came back, the one that made him feel like he was somewhere else, and he saw Ana, the cat he had whittled in her hand.

"Ana," he whispered, dazed with joy.

She held out her hand and he took it, feeling like he might float away.

The cedar smoke filled his senses as the feather touched his cheek- Butler's voice saying things he was beginning to recognize in his heart.

"Where are we going?" he asked, and he heard his ma's voice as if from far away, answering him and he wondered if she knew what was happening, wondered if Butler was beside her, holding her hand like he held Ana's, kissing her like he had Ana that day in the woods.

"The lanterns have been lit," Ana said. "But I will not find my way home."

He shook his head. "No."

"You were always so kind to me, Cal. And I used to think about what sort of man you would grow into, and what sort of woman I would become."

"Ana,"

"I thought about the homestead we might make together, thought about our children growing strong in the shadows of the oak trees, thought of the day they would have children of their own."

Cal felt heat gather in his cheeks and squeezed her hand.

"I did, too."

She put her finger to her lips, turned in a way that made her skirt fly out around her legs and he had no choice but to follow her into the darkness that seemed to swell around them.

The shadows lengthened, the light from the lanterns growing brighter as Ana led him on, the river rushing by their feet and Cal remembered how it felt to be in the water, remembered the man who looked like Andrew Karsten turning at the sound of his cry.

"It's close now," she said, and Cal looked again to the river, recognized it as the deadfall close to the Karsten Farm where the trees had blown over in a spring storm. He had gone there with Andrew to fish for salmon in the still pools. And later, during the hot summer days, with Butler as he taught him how to catch them with his hands.

"I know where we are," he said and, in the distance, he heard his mother answer but could not understand what she said.

"Are you sure?" Ana asked, turning again and Cal saw something around her neck, something he hadn't noticed before.

The circle intersected with the cross.

He drew a sharp breath. "Where'd you get that?"

She smiled, touched it with her fingers.

"I found it," she said, and Cal knew she was lying, knew that the tonic and the eagle feather and the drums were making him see things that had always been hidden.

"Ana," Cal said, reaching out to touch it himself. "That belongs to Justine."

"Are you sure?" she asked.

He frowned, not understanding. "She was wearing it when I found her."

Ana shook her head. "She took it from you."

"No," he said again. "I've never seen it before."

She smiled. "Don't you understand where she has come from?"

He took a step back, bewildered, and then she smiled again, looked down and Cal followed her gaze, saw something tangled in the branches where dead leaves made the water slow and thick.

His heart froze over at the sight of two yellow braids, the red ribbons that had been tied to the ends stripped away.

"Ana!" he cried, rushing towards the water, plunging in as he took hold of her arm, turning her over.

Her face was blue, her lips parted and her eyes, open and unseeing, seemed to be coated in a gray film.

"Ma!" he screamed, stepping away, tripping over the branches, feeling the leaves cup his elbows as he fought against the cold water that seemed to puncture his bones. "Ma!"

He heard her voice again, felt the eagle feather just brush the edge of his ear as something grabbed hold of his foot under the water. He yanked his leg, tried to break free as bony fingers clasped his ankle, a head rising from the river in front of him.

Cal felt his mouth open as two black eyes rose above the water, followed by a face he knew only too well.

"P-Preacher," he gasped as the head continued to rise. And then he saw the face, saw the skin of his cheeks hanging from bone as the man smiled at him.

The next moment he cried out as two strong hands eased him up by the shoulders.

"Oshkinawe," Butler said, very gently. "You are safe now."

Cal blinked hard, watched as Butler and his Ma came into sharp focus. They were sitting beside his bed, their chairs pushed together, a fire roaring on the hearth behind them, filling the room with a warmth that eased the ache in his head.

"Cal," his ma said, touching his hair. "What did you see?"

The boy blinked again, looked around the room and knew the monster of his dreams would be returning soon. Terror filled his chest as he imagined the preacher bursting in on his ma, demanding to know what was going on.

"Ma," he said, his voice shaky as he thought about the face again. "The preacher..."

She looked at Butler, her brown eyes worried for a moment. "He brought you here and then went to look for Ana. I told you this before,"

"No."

"Rest easy, Oshkinawe," Butler said, his voice soothing as he leaned closer. "No one is going to find me here. Your ma has pulled the latchstring and I am as quiet as a deer in the wood."

Cal felt his shoulders relax. He had watched the man pass through the forest without making a sound and in that moment, he remembered the deadfall and the blond braids ripped of their ribbons.

"What did you do to me, Nibwaakaa?" he asked. "I saw things on the table, the things we found in the woods, and I saw Ma," he paused. "She was *doing* something with them."

He watched Butler nod as though everything was exactly as it should be.

"Those are the totems," he whispered. "And they live inside of you now."

Cal took an unsteady breath and touched the back of his head, surprised to find the pain had gone.

"They will protect you and your children. No one will ever hurt you again."

"No one?" he asked, thinking of Preacher Younts and the face rising slowly from the river.

Butler nodded. "You are safe."

"Justine," he said suddenly. "Ana said her necklace belonged to me."

He watched his ma and Butler exchange looks; the confusion he had expected replaced with understanding.

"And I saw Preacher," he said, his heart still pierced by the image. "He was coming up out of the water... he grabbed me."

His mother glanced sharply at the shaman.

"Trust yourself, Oshkinawe. And tell us what we must do."

The boy took a breath. "We need to go to the deadfall by the Karsten Farm."

"Why?" his mother asked.

Cal swallowed, grief streaking his face. "Ana's there."

CHAPTER

FIFTEEN

I t took almost an hour to reach the place where Cal had been discovered, and I found myself looking up into the sky, watching the moon as it traveled above the trees.

My companions were silent, their movements measured as we made our way through the forest.

As we came near the river, I saw the line of lanterns placed on the edge and was reminded of all the things I had yet to learn about this place and the people who called it home.

I closed my eyes, willing myself to find Dylan like I had the summer before and felt my ankle roll, the sharp leather of my shoes digging into my skin and sucked in my breath.

"Is it the shoes again?" Jamie asked, suddenly at my side.

Pulling my skirt up, I examined my ankle and was surprised to find a raw band that was just beginning to ooze blood.

"Yes," I whispered, irritated that we had to stop because my feet didn't fit into a stupid pair of old-timey shoes. "I don't think I can walk in these anymore."

Jamie bent down beside me and held his lantern close.

"Pa," he turned to his father. "Can we spare a pair of ma's old shoes? Johnny burned up her old ones."

"Mayhap."

Jamie looked at me, obviously caught off guard.

"It's high time I start thinking about the future instead of the past."

I looked at him sharply as a cold thought entered my mind, one in which he returned to the cabin to find my grandmother in the arms of the man she loved.

"Seems I might need to make room for a new set of belongings soon enough."

I glanced at Jamie, saw the same troubled look on his face I wished I could show on mine.

"Pa?" he began. "What're you talking about?"

"You blind, boy?" his father barked. "Or can't you see what's in front of you?"

"I don't understand,"

"I intend to make Odessa my bride."

Jamie opened his mouth, shut it again and put a hand to the back of his head.

"But not before I have a proper ring to give her."

Jamie looked at me, his face suddenly white.

"You don't mean Ma's?"

The preacher grunted something, looked down at the earth while stroking his chin.

"I do not. And it's all for the best," he paused. "Tell me who would consent to wear another woman's ring?"

"Ma wouldn't have wanted anyone else to have it."

I heard the preacher make a sound low in his throat. "I believe you are right as she made certain it would never be found."

Jamie stood, a cold look in his eye.

"You don't know what happened, Pa. She could have taken it off or left it somewhere."

Henry Younts looked up at the sky, a vacancy in his eyes that made him seem lost.

"We were never without them, Son. And we quarreled that day."

"That doesn't mean,"

"I've spent enough time searching for things that will never return to me."

I felt my stomach turn over, a damp sweat gathering around the collar of my dress even though the night was cool. I imagined this man proposing to Odessa, imagined the joy it would give Louise and prayed my grandmother had the strength to refuse him.

"We need to keep moving," I said quickly, and Jamie nodded, his distress written plainly on his face.

"Loosen the laces of your boots," he said. "I'll bring the other pair tomorrow."

I smiled my thanks, did as he instructed before we trudged on, the night seeming to go on forever as the cries of people still searching met our ears.

"It's not far," he said. I felt my heart begin to beat faster, the thought that Dylan might be close making me breathless.

As if reading my thoughts, Jamie said, "If we can't find him, he most likely went to town."

I turned to him, disturbed.

"And since Johnny is gone and Louise will not leave her house after dark, it falls on me to take you there."

"You would do that?" I asked, our bond burning brightly in my memory.

He gave a quick nod as his father stopped short and pointed at a moss-covered stump.

"I found the boy right there, all alone aside from the ghost he says pulled him from the river."

I froze, my heart pounding in my ears.

Jamie stepped closer, handed the lantern to me and I bent close to the ground, shoving leaves and sticks aside, not sure what I was looking for.

I stayed that way for several minutes, wondering if Dylan had placed his foot here, or if he lingered by the stump, wondering which way to go when he heard Cal's cries coming from behind.

I wondered if he was frightened or confused- if he even knew I was alive.

I took a deep breath to calm myself and searched my memory for the last time I'd seen him. I'd been kneeling, my hand wet with blood when our eyes met. He'd shouted my name, one hand gripping the Whisper Stone as he fought to get to me.

I pressed my lips together, trying to imagine the terror he'd felt when I vanished before his eyes.

"Nothing to see," Henry Younts said, and I tightened my shoulders, ready to argue because if Dylan had been here, he would have damn well left something behind.

"Just a minute," I said, my hands sweeping the grass, my heart trying to feel where he had been when something cold brushed my fingers.

At once I pushed the underbrush aside, frantic as Jamie bent down beside me.

"What is it?" he asked, and I set the lantern aside, searching with both hands now.

"There," Jamie said, and in that instant, something gleamed in the firelight.

"What's that?" Henry Younts asked as I scooped it up.

"Looks like a coin," his son answered. "But what's on the front?"

I covered the picture with my thumb, turned it over and looked at the date.

"It's his," I choked. "It's Dylan's."

"How do you know?" Jamie asked, reaching for the coin and I pulled it away.

"I just do," I whispered, my hands shaking as I thought about

Dylan kneeling in this place while Henry Younts called for Cal, searching in his pockets for something he could use.

I held the quarter against my skin, wondering if it had come from the gas station he liked to stop at before work. Had he gone in for a coffee or a Coke or a Kit Kat, dumping the change in his pocket as an afterthought, never imagining how this one coin would change everything?

"He was here, then," Jamie said, his eyes still questioning as he stood with the lantern. "But which way did he go?"

"Probably headed to the tavern same as every man who is-" Henry Younts began.

"There's another one!"

I spun in a circle, saw Jamie pointing and fell to my knees.

"It's a penny," I said, picking it up before he could see what it looked like.

Another coin gleamed in the distance, and I crawled to it, confident now that Dylan was leading me somewhere.

"He's heading away from town," Jamie said. "And most likely towards the Cook place if Cal told him she was there."

I felt my hope ignite, praying Dylan knew where to find me.

"Why didn't he stay and help me care for the boy?" Henry Younts asked. "What sort of man runs off like that?"

"A man who's scared of something," Jamie answered. "But what would that be?"

I stood suddenly, anxious to divert their attention.

"When we find him, you can ask him yourself," I said. "Until then, I'm following the trail he left for me."

The two men stood watching me in the lantern light, neither moving until Henry Younts said, "Take her home, Son. I need to get back to Dess."

I straightened my shoulders, fear overtaking me.

"You said you'd search for Ana."

He crossed his arms against his chest. "It's not right her being at my place alone."

Jamie seemed to sense my discomfort. "You left the rifle."

His father grunted, shook his head.

"She's a good shot, Pa. She'll be all right."

He grumbled something, shook his head.

"You have to keep your promise," I spoke up. "It's the only way she'll trust you."

Henry Younts rubbed at his chin, struggling with a dilemma he'd brought upon himself.

"All right," he turned to his son, his voice like gravel in a creek bed. "But you take her home straight away."

Jamie nodded.

"And when you find her man," the preacher said, his eyes on me. "Tell him I'd like a word with him."

CHAPTER

SIXTEEN

"Did you find the boy?" Louise Cook pulled the door open as Jamie Stoddard and I climbed the steps of the front porch, and I knew she'd been watching from the window.

"Yes, ma'am," he answered. "Pa found him on the riverbank and he's resting at our house. Odessa'll bring him back in the morning."

Louise put a hand over her heart, held it there and closed her eyes. The next minute her lips were moving in a silent prayer, and I waited until she had finished before speaking.

"Cal says a man who looked like Dylan pulled him out of the water. I was hoping he'd been here already."

Louise shook her head.

"I've seen no one since Johnny joined the search this afternoon. Although someone should have told me my grandson was safe. I've been a worried mess."

"I'm sorry, Mrs. Cook," Jamie said. "We were busy tending to Cal."

She nodded; her movements abrupt as she held out an arm to me.

"Get inside quickly. There's a chill in the air."

I pushed down my protest and moved towards the door, my eyes scanning the yard for any sign of Dylan.

"We were just headed to town to see if her beau was there."

I turned to look at Jamie, felt Louise tighten her grip on my arm.

"You'll do nothing of the sort," she lifted her chin. "If that man of hers is wandering around town at this hour, you send him our way. Tell him to knock six times very quickly and we'll open the door. Otherwise, she's off to bed for a sound night's sleep."

"Louise," I began, wanting to protest but knowing the chances of finding Dylan were much better if I stayed put where Cal had told him I was.

She held up a hand, shuffled me inside. "Thank you for bringing her home, Jonas. You and the others will be in our prayers tonight as you search for the girl."

'Ma'am," he said.

"Goodnight." she shut the door in his face, her wide skirts swirling as she turned to me.

"Aren't you a sight," she scolded, her hands on her hips. "You could have caught your death out there and then we'd have nothing to give your man but a cold, dead body when he does take it into his head to fetch you."

I clasped my hands in front of me, the unlaced boots begging to be kicked off.

"I'll just wash up before bed," I offered.

"How's the boy, then?"

"He has a bump on his head. But he's resting now. Odessa didn't want to move him until morning."

Louise nodded. "Thank goodness Preacher was there. Maybe this will change that fool girl's mind about what sort of man he is."

I stood awkwardly, wanting to rebuke her reasoning while the sick feeling that time was running out continued to consume me. I couldn't just lounge around while Dylan was looking for me and Henry Younts was planning to pop the question to the woman who had spent the better part of the night invoking the power of the totems I'd come here to destroy.

Wiping at my forehead, I felt my wound pulsate to the beat of my heart.

"I'll go lie down."

Louise fixed me with a stare. "And no going out of doors no matter what you hear. Johnny told me he caught you with the rifle the other night."

I nodded, trying to look like a good girl as Louise shuffled off to her chair.

Moments later I was in my room and stripped down to a sheer white chemise that hung loosely around my shoulders. Lifting the bottom past my waist, I examined the bandage Odessa had changed that morning before we left for the market.

It was stained with sweat and blood that had oozed through the binding.

The bedside table had a clean roll of cloth and some iodine sitting on it, and so I began to unwrap the bandage.

Gritting my teeth, I pulled the cotton away from the sticky wound.

Pain punctured my breath and I gasped.

The next moment I was pouring the liquid on the welts, wincing as caustic pain radiated up my side before replacing the old cloth with new.

Once done, I spared a glance at the table. A pitcher of water was placed neatly beside a bowl- a handkerchief beside it.

Pouring out the water, I soaked the cloth and wiped it across my face and the back of my neck. I smiled; the feeling almost as good as an honest to goodness shower.

Placing the bowl on the floor, I stuck my feet in and leaned back, relief radiating up my feet and legs, erasing all other thoughts. Minutes later I reluctantly pushed it aside and slid beneath the covers of the bed I had come to consider my own.

I lay in the waiting darkness for some time, thinking of what to do.

I had to get out of bed and look for Dylan, had to force my aching feet and burning muscles to move even though Louise had forbidden it because if morning came and I still hadn't found him...

I pushed that thought aside, imagining instead what I would feel when I first saw him, the past three days reduced to a moment as I kissed him over and over again.

I turned my face into the pillow, undone by the image and how desperately I wanted it to be real, and if something happened to keep me from it-

"Muffet."

I gasped before I could help it, my fingers gripping the covers.

I heard the wind outside the window as it moved through the pines.

A figure came forward and I sat up quickly, my fear piquing even though I knew who it was.

He came closer, his long hair tied back as it always was, the canvas shirt he wore when he went fishing open at the collar.

"Dad," I whispered, not sure if I was dreaming. Not caring if I was.

"I'm here, Muffet."

I threw back the covers and my father backed away, put his hands up as if to stop me.

"Don't come any closer."

"What?" I asked, my heart breaking. "*Dad-*"

"I'm just a ghost here."

"No, "I shook my head. "You're not."

"Nothing ties me to this place."

I fought my panic, fought to stay seated in my bed. "I need you to stay. I don't know what to do."

"I can't stay, Muffet. And I can't come back."

I felt my throat tighten in disbelief.

"You made the path," he said. "Now find the stars."

I looked at him, trying to understand what he meant even as Adam's words came back to me.

"They'll take you home."

I swiped at my tears again. "I can't go home, Dad. Not without Dylan."

"He'll find you."

I drew a shallow breath,

"He just needs to see you."

"See me?" I asked.

"Like the eyes that saw you in the night," he said, moving backwards and I stood up, took a step towards him.

"Dad,"

"I love you, Muffet," he said. "And I trust you."

I stood, frozen to the spot, unable to remember the last time he had said that to me, knowing I had always felt it as an image of the wolf came to mind.

I'd been in the yard with Johnny, arguing about what I'd heard.

I threw a shawl over my shoulders, crept out of my room, and tiptoed towards the door.

Louise slept in her chair by the fire, her soft snores and the bottle in her lap telling me she would not hear the six fast knocks should Dylan happen to find the house.

I imagined the shock he would feel if Jamie did find him, wondered if he would willingly follow him to the house as I opened the front door, careful not to step on the squeaky board that warned the family every time someone came to call.

A few hurried steps and I was outside, the cool air toying with my hair as it fell over my shoulders, my side still burning despite the iodine and I took a faltering step, trying to remember where I'd seen the wolf.

Looking up again, I recognized the spot near the edge of the woods and hurried towards it.

One moment turned into a minute, and then another as I stood, wondering if I had mistaken my father's words for something entirely different. I watched as the moon peaked over the pines and touched my necklace.

A figure moved in the darkness, and I started, wishing for the rifle again.

"*Dylan?*" I whispered.

The figure stepped towards me, and I saw the moonlight glance off a pair of glasses.

"*Doc?*" I gasped. "What are you doing here?"

He took a step towards me, his movements sloppy and I smelled liquor on his breath.

"Just taking a walk," he said slowly, and I hesitated before taking a step back.

"A walk?" I repeated, and he nodded.

"I wanted to check on my patient," he rasped. "I have not seen you in the last few days."

I raised my chin, pulled my shawl tightly around my chest, hoping he couldn't see through the chemise in the moonlight.

"So, you sneak out here in the dark and spy on me?" I said, my temper flaring. "Why don't you just stop by tomorrow?"

He laughed, waved his arm over his head. "I think you know."

I took another step backwards. "No, I don't."

"Something strange is afoot here."

I felt a chill sweep my skin. "What are you talking about?"

He stood straight; his tone suddenly serious. "The moon is full. And a girl has gone missing."

"I know."

"You have stirred things up a bit here."

I gritted my teeth, furious to be taken away from my search for Dylan.

"I don't know what you mean. I simply came here for help and the Cooks were kind enough to give it to me."

He laughed again, shook his head. "The lanterns have been lit, even though the only child to ever return grew into the dimwit you see running this farm."

"Johnny?" I asked, my eyes widening. "What,"

"Shhhhh," he said, one finger to his lips as he took another unsteady step towards me. "I shouldn't have said that."

I crossed my arms, more annoyed than frightened. "You're drunk."

"You're right on that count," he said. "Went to the tavern after I left Preacher's because I can't stand that pile of sawdust the folks in this town gave me for a house. Not to mention the women here are not nearly as good-looking as was promised. Not that I haven't tried to make do-"

"You need to go home and sleep it off," I jabbed my finger at him, no longer a pioneer girl looking for vengeance, but a barmaid who had cut off her fair share of roughnecks.

He didn't move, just reached up and grabbed my wrist, his fingers running over the knotted flesh that had marked me since the summer before.

"I always wondered what these were," he said. "I saw them when I was tending to you, and I thought you might have done something to yourself. Thought maybe your beau had done something to you and that's why you ran away."

I yanked my hand free.

"How *dare* you!"

He laughed again, his face close to mine. "I'll tell you, but I want something in return."

I pushed at him, praying my strength would return but he stood in place.

"I want a kiss."

At once I began to panic, wondering if the medicine was fully awake now and what the hell Odessa and Butler had been doing in the cabin all night long.

"Just a kiss," he breathed, his lips just grazing my cheek. "And I'll let you go."

I pushed again, "No."

"Stop it," he said, his anger building as his arm rose in the moonlight and I knew he had every intention of hitting me.

I thought of Stumpy on his barstool, and No Name pinning Iris to the wall as I reached from behind to pull him off. Then I was running through the woods after Ethan, breaking the window of his car out with my elbow as I braced my back against the pine tree that had trapped Troy.

I felt my anger rise, desperate for the strength that had come to define me as I struggled in his grasp.

A sharp noise that sounded like flesh connecting with Doc's gut startled me and I watched, horrified as his body rolled away into the darkness.

Then I was lurching backwards, the shawl falling off my shoulders to tangle at my feet as Doc's attacker approached.

"Who are you?" I whispered, backing up against a tree, the panic I'd felt replaced by euphoria as Dylan stumbled into open moonlight and fell at my feet.

CHAPTER
SEVENTEEN

"Justine," I heard him say, my name on his lips the most beautiful sound I'd ever heard, and I felt my knees go weak, felt him come towards me.

"Dylan?" I asked, my hand reaching out even as my fingertips brushed the front of his shirt.

At once he pulled me into a crushing embrace, his face in my hair and I realized he was crying, realized I was crying as I collapsed against him.

"You're alive," he whispered, his hands running down my back and arms and over my shoulders, his lips finding my forehead where he seemed to pause, his whole body shaking. "I didn't know. I saw the blood and then…"

I put my hands on either side of his face, unable to speak.

"You disappeared," he continued, his hands in my hair again, taking the strands between his fingers as if trying to assure himself that I was real.

"I'm here," I whispered, my breath so shallow I thought I might not be able to take another one. "I'm okay."

He paused, pulled back to look in my eyes.

"I stood on the Whisper Stone again, but it didn't work. I had to keep trying over and over... until I was too exhausted to think about what might be happening to you."

"But you got through," I said, thinking of what Sara had said, holding him as though he would vanish at any moment. "I kept hoping you'd find me but then a day went by and then another and-"

"It's okay," he whispered, pulling me against him again, his hand cupping the back of my head.

A moment might have passed, or a minute or an hour. I'd lost all sense of time as he held me, the familiar planes of his body promising safety when nothing else could.

"I woke up by the river," he said. "And there was a boy who looked like Adam-"

"That's Calvert Cook," I nodded.

"He said you had a necklace like mine, said that his mother was taking care of you and that's when I knew where to find you."

"I'm so sorry," I said, my voice shaking, thinking of what he had been through even as I vowed that we would never be separated again.

"Don't say that," he whispered, and I buried my face against his chest, the sound of his heartbeat in my ear.

Then he pulled back, took my face in his hands, and kissed me, long and deep and hard, his need as raw as my own until a soft groan from the underbrush diverted our attention.

I turned and saw Doc's slumped body move in the moonlight.

Dylan had bloodied his lip and nose, knocked his glasses off his face where they lay glittering a few feet away.

"Who is he?" Dylan asked.

"He's the town doctor. And he's drunk."

"Why was he out here?"

I touched his face, still unable to believe that I was talking to him, and he was listening to me, helping me figure out what to do.

"He took care of me when I was shot," I paused. "I heard a noise and came out here, thinking it was you and then he grabbed me."

I heard Dylan mutter something under his breath.

"I tried to fight him off but..." I stopped. "I couldn't."

"Justine,"

"I can't *do* that here."

I felt his arms tighten around me.

"It's okay."

"No, it's not."

"Hey," he said softly, touching my chin with his index finger. "Rescuing damsels in distress is my job, remember?"

I smiled, his humor easing the last of my fears.

"And you sure as hell don't give me many chances."

I laughed, kissed him again even as my mind turned to the house and what awaited us there.

I thought about Odessa and Cal, thought about Butler and the place he had chosen for his own, a small cabin I'd seen on my way to market.

"You're shaking," Dylan said. "We need to get inside."

I nodded, wrapped the shawl around my shoulders even as the primal heat of a physical reunion began to build in my belly.

"This way," I whispered, and he looked at me, the same need in his eyes as I pulled him behind me.

"Where are we going?"

I turned, the sight of him making my heart scatter and thought about all the questions I should be asking, knowing they would have to wait.

"The Rook Cabin," I said, my skin on fire as I thought about what would happen between us there. "Butler uses it. But he won't be back until morning."

"Butler?" he asked.

I turned, silenced him with a kiss and the next second he deepened it, his mouth opening to mine before I pulled away, my feet moving soundlessly through the bitter grass.

It didn't take long to reach the shack, and I was surprised to see a glow coming from underneath the door. Stealing a glance through the window, I saw a fire burning in the hearth, one Butler must have built before he went looking for Cal and turned to the man I loved before ushering him inside.

"Justine..." he said again as I shut the door behind us, my hands in his hair as I pulled his face to mine. At once I felt his body begin to shake, felt his breath come in heavy rasps and pulled away.

He stood in the low firelight, still dressed in the khaki shorts and blue t-shirt I remembered and touched the lace at the collar of my nightgown.

"Seeing you like this," he whispered. "It's like you're not real."

"I'm real," I said, my hands gliding up the front of his shirt.

"I'm not dreaming?"

I smiled, my hands guiding his as he gently pulled on the ribbons that opened the front of my chemise. "You tell me."

The next moment he was pulling it off my shoulders, kissing the skin he'd just uncovered, and I was reminded of the first time we'd made love in his bed at the lake house. He'd been so tender, so passionate and I felt my head fall back against the door as his mouth traveled down my throat and over my breasts.

Kneeling in front of me, he let my nightgown puddle at my feet. At once he stopped.

"My God," he whispered, and I looked down, saw that the bandage I'd wrapped earlier had slipped to reveal the angry peppering of buckshot just above my hip. "Henry Younts did this to you?"

I nodded, felt his fingers splay across my stomach even as he tried not to touch it.

"I'm going to kill him with my bare hands."

I looked down, thinking he might get his chance, and saw a

small cot pulled close to the fire. I thought about my grandmother and wondered if she and Butler had shared this place in the same way.

Then I was pushing off the wall, desire numbing my senses as we made our way towards the hearth.

I touched the cot, ran my fingers over the heavy blanket that covered it and laid down. I heard Dylan's breath catch as he glanced at the door before dropping down beside me.

Then he was shrugging out of his clothes, and I had the absurd thought to burn them as Johnny had mine, wondering if we could find anything that would fit him.

"You're smiling," he said, his hands in my hair as he brushed it back from my face.

"You're here."

He paused, touched my cheek with his fingertips.

"Will I hurt you?"

"Dylan,"

"Will I?"

I paused. "You'll hurt me more if you don't."

He smiled, his thumb brushing my bottom lip as he looked into my eyes and I gazed at him, long and lean and beautiful in the firelight.

I whispered his name, the feel of him against me, and then inside of me, bringing a kind of completion that could only come in this way.

And as I laid beneath him, my hands on his shoulders as he sought a rhythm I recognized, I feared that he would be taken from me, that I would somehow be punished for what I had come here to do.

But he was here, his staggered breath telling me how I made him feel and it was almost too much, having him gone and then restored so suddenly that I feared any change might cause him to vanish again.

And so, I held onto him, my fingers tangling in the damp hair at the nape of his neck, my chest pressed so tightly to his I could feel his heartbeat.

And I prayed, my thoughts like a chant and knew I would rather live in this alien place forever than return home without him.

I tensed, my thoughts unclear and for an instant he stilled, pulled back.

"What is it?"

I couldn't answer.

"Justine,"

I looked at him, my voice barely a whisper. "I love you."

He smiled, one hand rising to cup my face as he dusted my lips with his own.

"I love you," he whispered. "And you're sure as hell not a dream."

I sighed, my hips rising to meet his and held his gaze, the blue and gray and silver I knew so well flecked with awe and surrendered to what had not only been building inside of my body, but my soul as well.

I KNEW it was foolish to linger in the Rook Cabin with dawn just brushing the sky, but I couldn't leave, couldn't abandon the warm nest Dylan and I had created in front of the fire.

And so, we talked, our voices lazy as I marveled at his presence, marveled that I could touch him and taste him and smell him, that I could look into his eyes and tell him everything that was in my heart.

Beginning with my brother.

"Where is he?" I asked after some time had passed, knowing his answer could change everything.

He leaned up on one elbow, touched my bare shoulder.

"He's hurt."

I tensed, felt him draw me against his chest.

"He got between you and Henry Younts," I said. "I told him to stay away, told him we couldn't be together in case something happened,"

"He loves you."

I felt tears prickle behind my lids, praying that my brother would survive, knowing I had to end this if I ever wanted to see him again.

"He'll be okay," Dylan assured me, his arms tightening. "Troy and Amanda will take care of him."

"Amanda," I echoed, thinking of the baby growing inside Sara Bennett, knowing she must have realized her presence here could tear the fabric we were desperately trying to hold together.

"She said there wasn't a place for her here, said your love would build a bridge so I could find you."

"And those quarters you dropped by the river didn't hurt, either." I smiled. "Nice work, Locke."

He chuckled. "Never thought my Three Musketeers addiction would come in handy."

"Guess I should stop complaining about the wrappers you stuff in the couch cushions."

He laughed, cupped my face again. "You can complain about anything you want."

I frowned. "Can I have that in writing?"

He smiled again, pulled me into another kiss and I wrapped my arms around his neck, wishing this moment could last forever.

Then he was rolling onto his back, settling me into the crook of his arm as we stared at the ceiling.

After some time had passed, he spoke.

"Troy told me not to come back without you."

I pressed my lips together, a strange tingle sweeping my body. "He did?"

Dylan nodded- not jealous- just acknowledging something he thought I should know.

"And Deputy Locke always gets his girl?" I asked.

He laughed. "Every century or so."

I smiled, content with the game we were playing even as the lightening sky told me it could end at any moment.

"Unless he's been playing basketball and crawls into bed without a shower."

He chuckled, shook his head. "That was *one* time."

"Once was enough!"

He chuckled again. "What do you think Holly and Dave would say if they could see us now?"

I smiled, the thought of our friends making them seem closer. "Holly would have every man within fifty miles doing her dirty work so we could stay in bed forever."

"Sounds good to me," he bent to kiss my shoulder. "But eventually you'd have to introduce me to your extended family."

I made a face.

"Come on," he teased, one hand behind his head. "I can do the yard work and you sew or knit or something."

"Or something..."

"No bills, no final exams, and no double shifts at Huffs. Sounds pretty sweet to me."

I laughed. "I kinda miss that last one."

"I'll give you Butt-head Brauski, but our crazy mothers can stay where they are."

I raised an eyebrow. "I hate to break it to you, but Odessa has one of those, too."

He chuckled, "She does?"

I nodded. "And even if she didn't, we couldn't possibly live in 1889. I burn everything I cook as it is."

"Then we'll eat out."

I giggled, our easy banter filling the places that had hurt for so long.

"Be serious," I said, only half joking and he raised himself up on one elbow, his hand seeking the side of my face.

"I was just getting to that."

I laughed again. "I wasn't serious... I mean. I want you to be *serious* but,"

He looked at me, his eyes searching mine with a strange intensity.

"What is it?" I asked, my heart beating faster, and he took my hand in his, turned my palm to his lips.

"I did a lot of thinking when I was trying to get back to you."

"You did?" I asked.

He nodded, "It shouldn't have taken a near-death experience to come clean about what happened at the Falls."

"Dylan,"

"I know you wanted me to open up to you."

"It's okay,"

"No, it's not. And I'm not making the same mistake twice."

I watched the pale morning light play soft against his skin.

"What are you talking about?"

He paused, touched my necklace with his finger. "I never told you where I was coming from the night we met."

I felt my senses awaken, wondering what could possibly remain unsaid between us.

"I was at the cemetery," he said, his eyes flicking away for a moment. "At Karen's grave."

I tensed; unsure I'd heard him right.

"It'd been a year and I was ready to start over," he paused. "And I knew that would never happen unless I let her go."

"Let her go?" I felt my pulse catch on itself.

"I said goodbye to her," he said, his voice low. "And then twenty minutes later you literally crashed into my life."

I held my breath, the love that had grown into something beyond us overwhelming me.

"It wasn't a coincidence we met that night," he said. "And

that's what kept going through my mind on the stone. I thought about what would happen if I never saw you again."

I nodded; my throat tight. "I thought about it, too."

He swallowed, his emotions overwhelming him.

"I wondered if I could go on without you," he said, "If I even wanted to and I made a promise to myself that when I did find you, I'd never lose you again."

"You won't," I shook my head. "I won't even make an Oreo run or fill up at the gas station without you. If I even had a car to fill up that wasn't smashed to bits or half dead already-"

"I know."

I looked at him, my heartbeat skimming like water on a windowpane.

"Marry me, Justine."

I felt my eyes widen, my face flush with wonder.

"Dylan,"

"I want to be your husband, want to wake up beside you in the morning and know that you're my wife."

I swallowed, unable to believe he was proposing in the middle of Butler's cabin as we lay naked in front of the fire.

And yet it seemed fitting.

"I want to see our kids playing in the backyard. Want to grow old with you on the front porch under those maple trees and I'm sorry it took me so long to figure that out."

I stopped him with a kiss, my hands tangling in his hair.

"Yes."

"What?" he whispered, pulling back.

"I said yes."

He smiled, the uncertainty I'd seen melting away. "You will?"

I laughed, tickled his side. "You sure know how to keep a girl waiting."

He squirmed. "It's common knowledge I can be kind of a meathead."

"No argument there," I laughed, not caring that the sun was

rising or that Butler might be returning, or Louise was probably fit to be tied.

He was mine.

And I was his.

And we would never be anything less to each other for the rest of our lives.

CHAPTER
EIGHTEEN

Cal had gone to sleep again, had breathed in the air that smelled of cedar and sage and felt his heart bend with a strange grief that had barely begun.

Ana was gone.

He was sure of that now.

But his mother and the shaman had given him something that would carry him into the rest of his life so he could start thinking like the man he would someday become.

Butler had gone to check the deadfall beneath the Karsten Farm just before daybreak.

His ma did not want him to go, had said the men would ask him how he knew, and smiled as he pulled her to him, kissing the top of her head as she laid it against his chest.

"I'll say I found Ana on my own."

"They'll never believe you."

"Dess,"

"They'll say I was the one who saw it. They hate me, hate that I love you and that's why we have to go away."

"Dess,"

"We have to find your people."

"No."

"Henry Younts wants to marry me. And Ma will insist upon it."

Cal watched as the shaman took his mother by the shoulders, holding her away from him while looking into her eyes.

"We will go away, Little One, but not to my people."

Cal felt heavy again and closed his eyes, listening as Butler told her a story about his clan and how they used to live freely along the shores of the lake they called Gichigami.

But those days had passed. His family had moved on and he did not know where they were.

"Why don't you find them?" his ma asked. "Why don't *we* find them?"

Cal wondered the same thing, thinking how wonderful it would be to leave the farm and journey to the northern woods in one of the birch bark canoes the shaman had talked about, and saw a sad look come into Butler's eyes.

"My name is no longer spoken."

A strange feeling came over Cal as a sound filled his ears like the buzzing of the June bugs in summer, and it made him dream again.

He saw Butler as a young man walking with the elders of his clan beside the Gichigami, learning the things he had taught Cal deep in the summer woods.

He watched as Butler made a fire, watched as a young woman joined him, her eyes holding the shaman's in a way that said she loved him.

Cal looked closer, wondering who she was, a heavy feeling in his stomach when he thought about Butler with someone besides his ma.

He watched as they left the fire and moved into the darkness-another person watching from the shadows.

Moments later the elders were talking with Butler. Then they were arguing as the shaman gathered his things and left the shores of the lake he called home, never knowing where his wanderings would lead him.

He remembered the scars on Butler's back and wondered if he'd gotten them when he was still a part of his clan, or if he had been beaten afterwards by someone who did not like the way he looked or the things he said.

And so, he became a man without a family.

Until he found them.

The thought made the boy smile even as he slept and he imagined them traveling to the remains of his old camp, moving past it and into the wilds of the north country.

And further... if need be.

Sunlight painted his eyelids, made him squint and he felt the heaviness that had surrounded him begin to lift, a lightness that hadn't been there before taking hold and Cal stretched his arms over his head, opened his eyes.

The room was bright, the sound of the June bugs gone and for a moment he forgot about Ana. His ma was standing by a window, looking out, her hands knotted at her waist.

She'd taken her braid out, her hair hanging in thick waves to the middle of her back and Cal thought how pretty she looked, wondering again who the strange woman standing beside the fire was.

At the sound of his movement, his mother turned.

"Cal," she said as he sat up in bed, rubbing his head.

"Did he find Ana?"

She reached out to touch his shoulder.

"I haven't heard anything yet, but Jonas Younts was here, Cal. He told me that his father plans to propose and I can't pretend that I love him, can't pretend that I want to marry him."

Cal looked down at his hands, wondering why she was telling him these things, knowing it had something to do with becoming a man.

A red line that had scabbed over on his palm caught his attention, and for the first time since he had awakened, he felt the stinging pain of it.

"Ma,"he asked, holding it up and her brown eyes softened.

"You and the shaman share the same blood now," she said. "The medicine belongs to your children, and your children's children."

Cal touched the scab, wondering if Butler had one like it.

"What about you?" he asked, suddenly worried. "How will you be protected?"

He watched her smile.

"He lives inside of me in a different way."

Cal looked at his hands again, thinking of the scars he'd seen running across Justine's wrists, the same scars that marked Butler and felt like he was climbing a hill, impatient for the view that awaited him.

"Ma," he said, his old life slipping away."When are we leaving?"

She turned, looked back out the window again.

"It must be when no one will miss us."

Cal thought for a moment, a picture of swirling skirts and shining boots painting a picture in his head.

"The barn dance," he said. "We could leave early and sneak away. Gran will be so tired afterwards she'll fall asleep in her chair and Johnny will go to the tavern like he always does."

His ma turned to look at him, her index finger tapping her chin.

"That's tonight."

Cal nodded, his thoughts turning to the wide fields and rich earth, to the rains that had come late in the season and the way the sun looked when it dipped below the horizon.

He remembered the sky the evening he'd found Justine and wondered what she would do when she discovered them gone.

"Ma," he said cautiously. "What about Justine?"

His ma turned back to him, nodded quickly as if trying to convince herself of something.

"Her beau is here. He'll take care of her."

Cal frowned again. "What if she can't find him? What if Preacher was right and I really did make him up?"

"You didn't."

Cal felt his heartbeat in his head, now.

"She should come with us."

"Calvert,"

"We can't leave her with Gran and Johnny."

His mother took a step towards him, her fingers working themselves into a frenzy.

"You don't understand, Son,"

"I think I do," he said, a strange commotion building outside as the June bug sound began to build again, rising to a crescendo that made his ears hurt and he put his hands up, cupped the back of his head.

HELP HER!

Cal felt the words in his mind, heard them in the same way he'd heard his ma talking and jolted on the bed.

Instinctively he looked around the room, searching for the speaker as his mother came to him quickly.

"Are you all right?"

"Did you hear it?" he asked, his heart pounding.

"Hear what?" she asked, clearly confused as voices rose outside.

Cal leaned forward, touched the lump on the back of his head and wondered if that was why he'd heard the voice, or if it had been the cedar and sage and eagle feather, the totems arranged on the table while Butler's blood mingled with his own.

He listened for the speaker again, felt the noise rise in his ears as a picture of a young boy swam before is eyes- his face like a mirror.

"Cal?" his ma asked again.

SHE'S MY SISTER

A knock on the door and Cal watched as his ma rose and fed the latchstring through, allowing the person outside to enter.

The next moment Preacher Younts was walking through, his large form blocking the sunlight as he stammered something about Ana.

Cal sat up straight, the pain in his head forgotten.

"Where is she?" he asked.

Jonas entered next and glanced at his mother as another man he knew only as Abraham Ebersole's brother stood in the doorway.

"She was found in the deadfall," Preacher spoke, his voice low.

"Henry," his ma said, touching the man's arm again and he heard Jonas clear his throat as he took another step inside.

"She's gone, Cal," he said. "I'm sorry."

"Gone?" Cal asked, not really believing it, thinking again of the silver necklace and the totems and the gift he made for her. He thought about the time one of their barn cats had died, remembered telling Ana about it as her eyes filled with tears and Cal had put his arm around her, wishing there was a way to bring it back.

And later, when he'd told the shaman, he watched as his face turn to stone.

"Do not wish for such things, Oshkinawe."

Cal had looked at Butler, wondering what he meant even as a dark thought began to settle in his mind, making him afraid.

"I wanna see her," he said.

The preacher's bushy eyebrows came together. "She's been taken to her home and you need to stay clear."

Cal shook his head, a fire burning in his belly.

"I'm going to see her."

He heard the preacher grunt.

"I suspect you'll do as I say."

DON'T FIGHT IT

He pushed the voice aside, had no room for it in the place where his skin began to burn hot with a rage he'd never felt before.

At once he threw the covers back, stood up and took a step towards the preacher.

The large man looked to his son, then to Abraham's brother.

"You going to disobey me, boy?" he asked.

"Henry,"his ma cut in. "Please,"

Cal watched the preacher turn to her, his face red. "I won't have it, Dess. If I am to be his pa, then I need to start taking him in hand."

Cal watched the color drain from his mother's face.

"Henry, "she stammered. "I don't,"

The large man turned in a circle, his cheeks blazed with shame.

"Surely you knew," he stammered. "That one day you would be my bride."

Cal watched his ma swallow, watched her pull her hair over one shoulder as though trying to hide from his gaze and felt the fire building inside of him, making him sweat.

He hated the preacher, hated the way he looked at him and spoke to him and bragged about making him a man when Butler had already done that a hundred times over.

But more than that, he hated that everyone thought he should marry his ma when no one had bothered to ask her about it.

"Dess,"the preacher repeated, almost helplessly.

He heard his ma clear her throat and took another step, saw their eyes move to him.

"She don't wanna marry you," he spat.

"What'd you say?" he grumbled, one meaty hand reaching for his shoulder, and Cal tightened up, pulled away even as his ma pushed herself between them.

"Don't touch him!"

Cal watched the preacher raise his hand, watched as his ma did something she'd never done before.

Rising to her full height, she grabbed hold of the preacher's wrist. The man began to squirm, his face red as he fought to break her hold.

"Ma," Cal said weakly, unable to believe what he was seeing.

"That Injun's magic has done something to you, hasn't it?" the preacher hissed. "I'll make sure he lives to regret it."

His mother's face contorted, her jaw tightening as she grabbed hold of his arm with her other hand. The next instant she pushed him, and he stumbled backwards, his boot catching the table as he fell to the side.

Time seemed to stand still while the others looked at his mother, then at him, their mouths moving in a way that made it seem like they were talking underwater.

RUN!

Cal stood rooted to the spot, not wanting to leave but knowing this might be his only chance to escape.

"Go, Cal!" his mother hissed.

He looked at her, sure now that the medicine was alive, and bolted out the door.

NINETEEN

"Well, don't you look like the cat that ate the canary," Louise Cook said as she met me on the front porch. "Who is this? Surely not your Dylan?"

"Yes, ma'am," he smiled, looking at me out of the corner of his eye before extending his hand, and I marveled at what this small gesture, what his very presence, meant to me.

And now that we were honestly engaged minus the modest ring I knew would come after we drained our savings account, I felt delight circling my shoulders like bluebirds in a Disney movie.

"Well," Louise said, clearly caught off guard. "Johnny has gone down to the barn looking for you and I was just about to try the river. You've been just about as much trouble as anyone has a right to be," she paused, her eyes on Dylan again.

"Ma'am?" he asked, and she cleared her throat, her cheeks red.

"You take after Andrew Karsten in the most remarkable way."

"Who's that?" Dylan replied, and I looked down, thinking he might have future in theater if the teaching gig didn't pan out.

"Our neighbor," she said while ushering us inside. "Are you related to his people?"

I watched Dylan scratch his head. "I'm not from around here."

"Hmmm," Louise mumbled, distracted. "I see Justine must learn to measure for your clothes."

I tried to suppress my amusement, remembering the moment we'd rummaged around in a trunk at the old Rook Cabin, a pair of brown cotton pants and a white shirt meant for a taller man were the only useful items we could find.

Once inside the house, Louise fixed him with another piercing stare.

"This is the second time I've opened my door to find her in the company of a man," she smiled. "But do not fret, Jonas Younts was simply offering her a safe escort home last night."

"Jonas Younts?" he said, and I looked away, wondering if his feelings for Jamie Stoddard still cut deep.

"The preacher's son."

Dylan nodded, the picture of perfect manners. "Then I'll try not to shoot him."

Louise huffed; her tiny eyes wide before shaking her finger at him.

"I see you are full of mischief, young man. And I am pleased to find you in good humor. Almost as pleased as I am to know you will be taking Justine with you. We have done all we can for her here."

He bowed slightly. "And for that I'm grateful."

I watched her smile, heard her clear her throat and knew he was getting to her.

"Happy to do it," she said. "But I'm also wondering how quickly you can collect her things and go. My grandson is expected home and he's in a bad way."

I glanced at Dylan, bit my lip because while I'd expected her to dump me like a hot potato, I hadn't expected it to be in the first three minutes.

"Heaven knows why he didn't go straight away to market with us like he always does," she paused, looked at me. "If you ask me, he was up to no good with that Cuppy girl and is now on the wrong side of it."

Drawing closer to her, I touched her elbow, lowered my voice.

"I'd like to take Dylan to the barn dance."

I watched her cheeks puff out, irritated with my request.

"Of all the foolish,"

"Penelope Karsten said she was most anxious to meet Dylan when I spoke to her at the Jennison Barn," I lied. "She hopes to visit Mackinac Island one day."

"Penelope Karsten?" Louise repeated, her eyes shiny. "She hasn't given me the time of day since that rascal ran off on Dess and the boy."

"Really?" I played along.

"And don't you think her girl Abigail fools me. I know she's playing the part when she comes here, spying on us, pretending she's a friend to my daughter and all the while gossiping how we do without when they've never known a day of want."

"Louise," I squeezed her arm again. "I think Penelope will be most interested in everything Dylan has to say, most interested in everything *you* have to say, since you nursed me back to health."

She waved her hand in front of her face. "Oh... I never stay long at these things."

Dylan came forward, smiled in a way that seemed to startle her.

"I'm happy to do an honest day's work, ma'am," he said. "To earn my keep."

Louise shifted her shoulders, considering his offer.

"And I promise I won't be any trouble."

She raised an eyebrow.

"I suspect you could be a great deal of trouble, young man, if you took it into your mind to do so," she paused, thinking hard on something as she bustled towards the table. "I wonder if you know your lady was found wandering around in her unmentionables."

Dylan glanced at me.

"Unmentionables?"

"Yes," Louise answered. "They were ruined, so Johnny burned them, and I hope you are not expecting me to pay for replacements as they are likely quite costly."

"No," Dylan smiled. "I can buy more.... unmentionables."

"Well, when you do, make sure her name is sewn into them," she huffed. "I was beginning to think she didn't have a beau and Victoria was the name of some lady she chose to lay with instead."

Dylan glanced at me again, no doubt aware of the misunderstanding as his eyes crinkled.

"I'll do that, Ma'am."

Louise nodded briefly, then stood on tiptoe, looking at something over our shoulders.

"Here comes Johnny now. He's to start cutting on the field border after dinner and will need help binding the shocks."

Dylan nodded, and I knew that even though he had no idea how to bind a shock or cut a field border, he would do whatever it took to stay in her good graces.

"It's later than I'd like but let's get you dinner and then find some clothes that are fit for field work." Another sideways glance. "It's strange for a man such as yourself to travel without a bag."

Dylan glanced at me, cleared his throat. "I left in such a hurry after hearing about the raid I must have forgotten."

Louise narrowed her tiny eyes again,one hand on her hip as her son came in the front door. "Strange we've had no news of it."

I touched her shoulder, turned her towards the kitchen.

"What is that wonderful smell?"

"It's ma's cornmeal mush and beans," Johnny spoke up from behind. "You must be her fella."

Dylan nodded.

"Thought you'd never show up."

"Son," Louise said quickly as they sat down at the table. "Dylan is going to help you today.

They are staying for the barn dance and Penelope Karsten has expressed her *keen desire* to meet him."

Johnny nodded, began eating and we followed suit, the silence punctured only by the sounds of silverware scraping metal plates and I met Dylan's gaze over the table, my small smile telling him everything would be all right.

I just needed to believe it myself.

It wasn't long before Johnny stood, waiting for Dylan to do the same. I watched him rise slowly, heard Louise order her son to give him some of his clothes and he nodded towards the loft.

Ten minutes later Dylan emerged looking ready to tackle the pioneer life we'd been forced to partake in.

"Don't work too long, Son," Louise instructed. "I expect Odessa and Cal any time and Dylan will need to change before the dance."

"Yes, Ma," Johnny said. Then, turning to Dylan, "Meet me in the field nearest that big cottonwood. I'll go fill our jugs from the well."

Dylan nodded, watching as the other man left, turning only when Louise clucked her tongue at him.

"The clothes you came in won't do at all now that I know Penelope wants to speak with you," she took a step back to look at him, patted her hair nervously. "I will look in my chest of drawers for some of Seth's things. They will do nicely."

"Ma'am-"

"Hush now," she clucked at him, smiling now. "It will do me good to see them put to use again."

Without another word, she hustled off with a distracted air and I stood alone with Dylan, who motioned for me to follow him outside.

Once on the porch, we watched as Johnny disappeared into the barn and I turned, shutting the door behind me.

"You heard what she said about Cal?" I whispered. "If I hadn't been here, Odessa would have made him go market instead of letting him see Ana. I'm already screwing things up, and the longer we stay, the worse it'll get."

He gazed out at the field and the large cottonwood tree growing beside it, his jaw working in the way it always did when he was worried.

"I say we find her at the dance tonight, take the medicine bag and get the hell out of here as fast as we can."

"She'll never give it to us."

I heard him draw a quick breath, clearly frustrated. "Maybe she won't have a choice."

"No," I said, my voice firm. "I can't do that to her. She'll be defenseless."

He shook his head, glanced at the barn again. "That's not our problem."

I felt my anger rising and put a hand to my forehead.

"It *is* our problem. You've never met her, never seen what her life is like."

"Baby," he said, his hand on my cheek. "You need to think about us."

I pulled away, walked to the end of the porch.

"I *am* thinking about us."

We heard a noise, saw that Johnny had shut the barn door, a pair of scythes over his shoulder as he motioned to Dylan.

"And even if Odessa does come to the dance and we can get our hands on the bag, what are we going to do with it?"

He shook his head. "I don't know. Try the reversal again minus you slitting your wrists and a psychotic preacher trying to kill me?"

"Dylan,"

"I'm not leaving here without it."

I took a breath, weighed my words carefully.

"But what if destroying the totems changes the reason we came together? You said yourself it wasn't a coincidence we met that night."

He looked at me, his eyes darkening.

"What if I lose you?" I continued, my thoughts spiraling. "And Adam... what if he's never *born?*"

"You can't think like that."

"I have to."

"There's no other way."

I shook my head. "There has to be."

"J,"

"Esther Ebersole made a home for the stars."

He put a hand on the back of his neck, turned in a circle. "What the hell does that mean?"

"I don't know, but Dad said they would lead us home."

He sighed, started walking down the steps and I felt my heart stop.

"Dylan,"

He turned at the bottom, his face shadowed, and I went to him, took his hands in mine.

"What is it?" I asked.

He looked down; his voice so low I could hardly hear it. "If we do this and everything changes, if we never meet or grow old together or watch our kids play on that swing set I'm going to build, then at least," he paused, took a quick breath. "At least we won't remember it."

I felt my breath stop. "What're you saying?"

"We have to end this, J. One way or another."

I stood, the late morning breeze in my hair, my legs made of rubber and gripped his hands for support.

"But-"

"I can't go on like this," he said, taking a step back. "You know that, right?"

I looked down, pressed my lips together as I squeezed his hands tightly.

"I'll make the path."

"What?"

"I'll find another way."

He looked at the cottonwood again, then down at his feet.

"I gotta go."

I stood still, my body trembling as he pressed his lips to my forehead.

Then he was walking towards the barn, following the same path Johnny had moments before and I hated what our words meant, hated that risking our past might be the only way to save our future.

I put my head down, took a slow breath, then another and another until I felt certain I could turn around and enter the house when a shadow passed in front of me, followed by the scent of lilacs.

I lifted my eyes.

A woman stood before me, her beauty a thing I'd only imagined.

"I hope I'm not intruding," she said, her voice as lovely as her face and I shook my head, wondering how a creature like her could ever impose on anything.

"Of course not," I managed, and she smiled- a luminous thing that made the sunshine dim around us.

"My name is Esther Ebersole," she bowed her head. "And I've been ever so anxious to meet you."

CHAPTER

TWENTY

"Y ou have?" I asked, unable to stop myself from staring at every nuance of her face, trying to piece together the mystery of this woman and why my life had fallen apart because of her.

I felt my gaze travel to her smooth cheeks, pausing at the blue eyes that seemed as still as a moonlit pond, all crowned by a mass of dark hair that would have snapped my neck in two.

She was clothed impeccably in a bustled silk saffron dress that complimented her coloring, crisp eyelet cotton at her bodice and cuffs.

She smiled, seemingly amused at my unease and at long last I understood why Jamie Stoddard had been driven mad by her death, knowing I would grieve her after only this brief encounter.

She smiled, climbed the steps, and for the first time I noticed that Sara Bennett lingered behind her.

"You are all anyone has been talking about for the past three days."

"I am?"

"It's not every day a lady survives a gunshot wound. And by

bandits, no less!" She turned to Sara, who would not meet my eyes. "I have also brought you some shoes, of which I hear you are in sore need."

"Shoes?" I repeated, feeling dumb because I had no words of my own as Sara placed them on the top step.

Esther laughed again, and I heard the front door swing open as Louise scurried up beside me, a wide smile on her mottled face.

"Mrs. Ebersole," she breathed. "What brings you here today?"

Esther turned, motioned to Sara. "We came to inquire about Justine, but I am also anxious for news of Calvert. We hear he has been found."

Louise pressed her lips together as she crossed herself. "Odessa stayed at the preacher's cabin to nurse him. We expect them home at any time."

"That's good news isn't it, Sara," Esther said, turning to the young woman beside her and I caught the latter's eyes, saw them dart away and wondered if she had been forced to come here because Esther wanted to run errands and needed someone to do it with.

"Yes," Sara said, looking down, her hands clasped in front of her. "Although Butler found the Cuppy girl in the deadfall this morning."

"No!" I heard Louise draw in her breath.

Esther nodded. "Word came to us early this morning. Abraham rode out straight away to see to the family."

"How terrible," Louise said, her hands suddenly smoothing her apron.

"It is," Esther agreed. "And were it not for the gentlemen from the railroad coming in today we might have abandoned the dance on account of it."

"The railroad?" Louise repeated. "Coming here?"

"We have high hopes," Esther said. "And Abraham is just the man to lead the way."

"Of course," Louise agreed. "Would you care to come inside for some tea?"

Esther shook her head slightly. "I have much to do today and Mr. Ebersole does not like me to linger out of doors. Although I feel so fine there is no reason for worry," she patted her hair, fixed me with another dazzling smile. "Come, Justine. Let's take a walk."

I looked to Louise, who seemed taken aback before lifting her chin and giving a quick nod.

I stood, waiting until she went back inside. The next moment Esther grasped my hands in hers, squeezed as if we'd been friends forever.

"Got rid of her, didn't we?"

I looked to Sara, who gave a shy smile as she walked down the steps.

"Is it true you have a beau who is sick with worry and wonders if you are even alive?" Esther asked, linking her arm with mine as Sara cut in front of us, a playful lilt to her walk.

"She mistook Andrew for him."

Esther glanced at me, a twinkle in her eye.

"That is high praise indeed. I am hopeful he will ask my girl to marry him."

"Esther!" Sara gasped and I laughed, thinking how much fun it would be to spend an afternoon with these women at Back Forty Farm, the horrible memories of my time there erased as we lingered beside the lavender field.

"You wish it, too," she scolded. "I see how you sneak off in the afternoons to walk by the river and come home with pine needles in your hair and on the back of your skirt."

"Hush," Sara whispered, her face ablaze and Esther waved her hand as though swatting a gnat on a summer day.

"Is it true that Odessa has been nursing you day and night, and that even Louise has given you medicine from her bottle in hopes you will recover in time for your beau to fetch you?"

"He returned last night," I said, Esther's hand tightening on my arm, and I was reminded of how much I missed Holly. "He's helping Johnny in the fields right now."

"How kind of him," Esther said. "The Cooks have done without for quite some time. Ever since the father died, really."

"Oh?" I asked, wanting to know more.

"You must have heard how he treated Johnny and Odessa as children, and about Louise and her *headaches*."

I looked at Sara, and she met my gaze, her eyes taking me back to Amanda.

"She takes that bottle everywhere she goes," Esther said. "There are times Doc won't give her any, so she travels under the pretense of calling on her sister to get more."

I felt myself leaning closer and Esther stopped, the cottonwood tree beside us and I looked to the field, suddenly desperate for a glimpse of Dylan.

"I'm certain you have seen her temper."

I squinted, the sun playing hide and seek behind the tall pines that lined the field.

"I have," I said, a memory stirring from the night before. "But there is one thing I wonder about."

Esther turned to me, her eyes making me believe there wasn't anything I couldn't ask her.

"I heard the lanterns once led a child home."

The two women glanced at each other.

"Was that child Johnny?" I asked.

Esther put a hand to her hair, lowered her voice as though he could hear us from the fields. "Odessa was two years older and always doted on Johnny, but one day when he was very young, he went hunting with his father. When Seth returned home, he told everyone that a large deer had stepped out of the woods in front of him. He stopped to shoot at it and swore the boy was right beside him, but afterwards, Johnny was nowhere to be found."

I felt my heart speed up, the wind holding its breath as she spoke.

"The lanterns were lit for the first time that night. Odessa remembered how her brother loved to touch the flame through the glass of the kerosene lamp and they thought, they *hoped* it would lead him home."

I took a breath, my thoughts tumbling towards a young Johnny wandering the darkened woods alone.

"For two days and nights everyone searched. Then, on the third night my husband's father was walking the bank, checking the lanterns just past the cedar swamp when he saw Johnny standing there, watching him from the other side of the river," she paused, her eyes haunted. "He called out to him, and he just stood there like he hadn't heard a thing."

I felt my body go still, hanging on her every word.

"It seems something happened to him in the woods, but no matter how many times he was asked, he was never able to tell anyone what happened."

I tightened my grip on her arm.

"Louise swears he was a normal child before, but I suppose we will never know," she shook her head, her tone grim. "Now you can understand why we were all so worried about you."

I pressed my lips together, gave a quick nod.

"We would have taken you in at the Farm, but I know very little of healing arts and Odessa has learned much from the shaman."

I looked at her, my smile faltering.

"I've ruined our walk, haven't I?" she asked, her lovely face shadowed. "Sara, you must stop me when I talk about unpleasant things. Although you're no better at holding your tongue."

Sara's forehead creased, perhaps embarrassed by Esther's appraisal as we turned and began making our way back to the house.

"You must be sure to bring your beau to the barn dance tonight," Esther said, her arm still in mine. "It is always such a grand affair, and we are so anxious to give you a proper send off."

I nodded, hoping my proper sendoff included a fast track to the future and an end to the curse that seemed to have been part of my legacy long before Jonas Younts ever stole the medicine bag.

"I will tell Abraham and he will make sure everything is perfect for you tonight."

I smiled my thanks, ready to slip in a question about the stars and what sort of home they might live in when the color drained from her face.

"Esther?" I asked. "Are you alright?"

She nodded, took a quick breath while reaching for a handkerchief she had hidden in the eyelet at her cuff. Pressing it to her mouth, she coughed, a small splash of blood staining the white material.

"Esther," Sara came closer, put an arm around her waist. "I told you this was too much."

She shook her head, the blood rattling in her throat as she tried to clear it.

"And all for what? A little gossip."

"It's nothing," Esther insisted, the cough catching her again as she fought for a second breath.

"Let me get Louise and we can hitch up Lolly," I offered, the handkerchief peppered with blood now.

"There is no need," Esther replied, her voice hoarse. "And there is nothing that can be done to stop what will happen."

"Don't say that," Sara cut her off. "Abraham just found a new doctor."

"My dear," Esther said, wiping at the corner of her mouth. "You know as well as I that no strolls by the lake or trips to the mountains will help. So, let me enjoy this day without making a spectacle of myself."

"You're not making a spectacle," I insisted, looking over my shoulder in the hope that Johnny or Dylan or even Louise might see us. "Can you make it to the house?"

She coughed again, gave a quick nod as we moved across the lawn.

One step turned to two, then three and four and ten as we shuffled towards the home of Louise Cook, a fact I felt sure would mortify Esther.

"Someone's in the yard," Sara said suddenly, and I looked up, the casual slope of the man's shoulders telling me all I needed to know, his steps crumbling into a run when he saw us.

Seconds later Jamie Stoddard stood before us, unable to conceal the passion he felt for the woman we supported between us.

"Jonas Younts," Esther managed, her shoulders straightening in the slightest as she fixed him with her most dazzling smile. "Whatever brings you here?"

CHAPTER
TWENTY-ONE

Cal ran so quickly he barely felt his feet touch the earth. And as he ran, he thought about Ana, thought about his mother and Butler. But most of all, he thought about the preacher and what he had said.

Surely you knew, Dess... that one day you would be my bride...

The thought made him sick to his stomach, made him fear what would happen if they weren't able to get away.

He knew his mother could handle Preacher; knew he would do as she asked because he was in love with her. But it wouldn't last forever, and if they could just make it through the barn dance tonight...

But until then, he would have to go home and pretend like he hadn't started a fight with a man four times his size, would have to say he was sorry if called to account, biding his time until they made their escape.

He thought all this as he ran, the sound of his footsteps the only noise in the forest as he took the path that led to the Cuppy Farm.

He came out of the trees and into a field, saw the house tucked against the side of a hill, a big sycamore tree in the front yard, barns spread around like building blocks on a worn blanket, and stopped.

Bending over, he put his hands just above his bent knees and tried to catch his breath, tried to scan the surroundings for anything out of the ordinary.

A beautiful horse he recognized as belonging to Abraham Ebersole stood tied outside and Cal knew he was seeing to the family because that's what the rich farmers did. He knew the Karstens would send someone as well even as they continued to prepare their home for the evening's festivities.

Cal allowed himself a moment to think about how Ana might have looked tonight, imagining the dress she might wear or the way they might smile at each other. He thought of her little sister tangling at her feet as their parents stood at tables filled with food.

He swallowed his sadness, watching from the trees as another sound carried across the fields. It was Preacher Younts atop his huge mare, the sound of her hooves beating the hard earth and Cal knew in his heart he was searching for him.

The preacher dismounted by the door, tied the mare beside Abraham's gelding as Mr. Cuppy came outside. At once they turned towards the tree line where he stood, their eyes shaded against the sun and he pulled back, afraid he would be seen.

Cal watched them talk in the yard and knew they were discussing him and how he had led Ana into danger, a sick knot forming in his throat seemed to yank on his stomach.

He needed to go, needed to get away from here and head home where he could begin gathering the things he needed for his new life and if his gran or Johnny or even Justine asked about it-

"Oshkinawe."

He turned, saw the shaman standing amongst a copse of hickory trees and had no idea how he'd gotten there.

But he didn't care, he ran towards the man and fell into his arms, tears spilling over his cheeks now.

"Nibwaakaa."

Butler went to his knees, pulling him close as he cupped the back of his head.

"I am sorry," he said. "It is difficult to lose what a young heart first wants."

He didn't say anything, just nodded into his shoulder.

"Ana is on another path, and as much as you would like to follow her, yours will be different."

Cal looked into Butler's dark eyes.

"We need to run away, Nibwaakaa. We need to get Ma and go away,"

"You must not say such things."

Cal pulled back and felt confusion overtake him.

"I did not say you should not think it, Oshkinawe, only that you should not *sait*," he said, his voice almost a whisper. "If others hear, they will watch you closely and keep us from going."

Cal smiled then, a true smile of joy, knowing that tonight would begin their journey into a life that was meant to be more.

"Are you ready?"

The boy paused, thinking hard on the question because no one had ever asked him that before.

"There's nothing left for me here."

Butler looked at him again, his strong hands squeezing the boy's shoulder. "That is not true. These are your people, even if you do not like what they do or the way in which they do it. And this is the land you have worked with your own hands. And these," he motioned to the hickories that towered around them. "Are the trees you have grown tall in the shadows of."

Cal looked up, heard the leaves rustle in the wind.

"This place will one day hold the remains of your ancestors, and because of that it will always call to you."

Cal looked at him closely, wondering if he was thinking about his own home on the shores of the Gichigami, where he had lived with the woman who stood beside him at the fire.

"Who was she?" he asked, suddenly and without thought.

Butler paused, then stood up slowly and looked down on him. "Who do you mean?"

Cal stood up straighter. "The woman who stood beside you at the fire. The one the others were arguing about."

He saw the shaman's eyes soften and knew he was not angry with him.

"The medicine has given you the eyes of an eagle, and through them, you see everything."

Cal remained still, ready to listen as the shaman looked back towards the Cuppy Farm and the rolling hills that surrounded it.

"She was a daughter of the chief, who was a friend of my father's. But she was young, and already promised in marriage to another from a different clan."

Cal watched him, wondering what they had meant to each other.

"We loved each other, Oshkinawe, but I do not want you to think it was the same love I feel for your mother. I was bold and reckless and had no thought of tomorrow, and in secret I took her away and made her my wife."

Cal's eyes widened. "Nibwaakaa,"

Butler held a hand up. "You must not judge me on the boy I once was. Just as others should not judge you by what happened on the riverbank."

Cal bit his lip, knowing he was right.

"We lived apart from our clan for the time she was with child. And when our son was born, he lived only a few hours before taking her with him into the afterlife."

Cal stepped back.

Butler had been married... with a son...

He felt his skin go hot with disbelief.

"I took her back to the village for burial and our clan brought moccasins and tobacco. They kept the fires burning for five nights while the young children wore charcoal on their foreheads. I tried to speak to her father, tried to explain why I had behaved as I had, but he would not listen. I was the clan's chosen healer, had learned the ways of the Midewiwin beside my father and grandfather and there was no excuse for my selfishness."

"Nibwaakaa,"

"My name was never to be spoken again and my sacred totems were taken from me. I was told to leave and never return."

Cal swallowed, a dull ache in his chest.

"But that was not enough for me, Oshkinawe. My heart was so heavy, my sorrow as sharp as the tip of my knife and so I asked the chief to strike my back eighteen times. One lash for each year of his daughter's life, and another for our son, who was buried in her arms in the sacred ground that still calls to me."

Cal felt his words, a strange buzz building in his head again and saw what Butler had told him, watching the stick fall across his shoulders, leaving the marks he had seen in the river.

And then he saw Justine again, saw the same white lines running across her wrists.

"My way was bitter and lonely until I found you and your mother. The Gichi- Manidoogave me another path, and I am not troubled by where it leads, because in this season I have spent with you, I have remembered."

Cal looked up, eager for more. "Remembered what?"

The shaman smiled, closed his eyes for a moment.

"What I am looking for."

Cal cocked his head, wondering what the shaman meant, knowing a lesson was about to begin and that all he needed to do was listen.

"Do you remember when you wished to bring the cat Ana loved back to life?"

Cal nodded.

"And remember when I told you not to wish for such things?"

"Yes."

"There was a time, after my wife and son were buried, when I longed for the same thing you do now."

Cal held his breath, wondering how the shaman knew what he was thinking.

"Two paths appeared in front of me. One led to a dark wood where the trees hunted the sun. The other led to the door of your mother's home, where I spent the first days of spring working the earth beside her."

Cal stood still, remembering the moment Butler had come into the yard and spoken to Johnny. The sky had been brilliant, the wind just beginning to warm as he led him to the place where his mother was kneeling, her hands raw from digging as she looked up at them.

Waiting, it seemed, for that very moment.

"You must choose your path, Oshkinawe."

Cal looked at him, seeing his bottomless eyes and beyond that, the boy who looked like a mirror.

"I heard something," he whispered, suddenly afraid, thinking of the dark wood Butler had spoken of.

The shaman stood still, waiting.

"It was a voice. And I saw a boy. He looked like me."

The shaman nodded.

"He told me to help Justine. He said she was his sister," he paused. "Who is he, Nibwaakaa?"

Butler looked down on him, then turned back towards the woods.

"Let us walk," he said. "I have much to tell you."

"Esther," Jamie Stoddard whispered, her name like a prayer. "Are you all, right?"

She looked up at him, the bloody handkerchief still in her hand, and tried to smile.

"No better or worse than any other day."

I glanced at Sara and knew she was worried.

"Would you like to go inside?"

Esther laughed then, a vibrant thing that seemed at odds with our circumstances.

"I'd rather die out here than let Louise Cook fuss over me."

"Esther," Jamie said again, his voice low. "Please don't say that."

She shook her head, took a few steps on her own as if to prove that the episode had passed.

"I only speak the truth, Jonas. You of all people should know that."

"Please," Sara said while circling to the front and taking her friend's hands. "Let Jonas take you back to the farm in his wagon."

Esther stopped, gazed at Jamie with a love she was no longer able to hide.

"I am perfectly fine now," she said, a tiny lift to her chin and I didn't doubt that she was, didn't doubt that this sickness caught her off guard which was why she carried a handkerchief hidden in the sleeve of her dress. "And while I don't wish to be carted off like a sack of potatoes, I would welcome a moment of rest in the shade."

I stood dumbly, watching Jamie who stood as if made of stone, his jaw working as Dylan's did in times of stress.

"Of course," he said, taking her hand and leading her to a nearby oak, her saffron dress billowing in a perfect circle as she sank to the ground and I looked at Sara, wondering if we should leave them.

"I brought that pair of shoes I promised," Jamie said, and Esther laughed.

"We are of the same mind, then. I also brought a pair and now Justine is positively spoiled."

She put her hand out, drew him down beside her and I stood

frozen, stunned by the gesture, realizing she either trusted me or had nothing left to lose.

I watched Jamie Stoddard relax in the slightest, watched a slow smile spread across his face and knew he'd never been happier in all is life.

"Come, Justine," Sara said, drawing me away and towards the side yard and I followed her, willing to give them this moment.

We walked silently into the backyard, which was empty aside from the wash that Louise had hung sometime during our walk.

"Sara?" I asked but she continued to move just ahead of me, stopping only when she had reached the side of the shed where we were hidden from the house.

"Okay," she spun to me, her voice a ragged whisper. "I've tried to convince myself that you're crazy, but I just can't do it."

"What?" I asked, my mind spinning for traction.

"You looked like you went into some weird trance on the riverbank,"

"Sara,"

"And I know damn well you don't get nosebleeds."

I held her gaze, willing her to continue.

"Is Andrew in danger?"

I tensed, ready for confrontation before realizing all she wanted was the truth.

"Yes."

She turned in a circle, her hands on her forehead.

"How do you know that?"

"I told you," I said slowly. "I came here on the Whisper Stone."

She shook her head, took a step away before turning towards me again.

"And you say... *I* told you this?"

"I know all about Daniel Calhoun and how he took you out there on his motorcycle," I paused, unsure if I should go fauther. "I even know about the baby."

Her eyes widened.

"You know what the Whisper Stone can do," I paused, let my words sink in. "I'm guessing you don't want to find out what it can take away."

She stood for a long moment, her breathing hard before peeking around the shed again and I felt bad for scaring her.

But not bad enough.

"Are Esther and Jonas planning to meet anytime soon in secret?"

She put a hand to her mouth, chewed on her fingernail.

"I know Mr. Ebersole is taking her to see a new doctor. He wants Esther to go west, and Jonas is afraid she won't come back."

"And she told you this?" I asked.

Sara nodded; her eyes glassy.

"When is she going?"

Sara looked at me, still chewing on her nails. "Sometime after the dance. Abraham's talking to the men about clearing land for the railroad and then,"

"You need to find out," I interrupted. "And then you damn well better tell me."

She shook her head. "I don't know if I can. Esther's mood changes every three minutes. You saw her-"

"You'd better figure it out," I said. "Because if you don't, there's a good chance your baby will never know her father."

I heard Sara gasp even as her face went white.

"*Her?*"

I paused, shaken by what I'd just revealed.

"Yes," I said. "Her name is Amanda."

"Amanda?"

"She's very kind. And brave-"

"Brave?" Sara said, the word a mystical thing that seemed to float away.

"And she's in love with a good man. They're going to build a life together."

Sara touched her face, her fingers moving as if my words were made of moonlight.

"But if you know her…" she stopped, unable to continue.

"She wasn't born here," I said, wanting her to know the truth. "Believe me when I say you can still get your happy ending."

She looked at me, her hands dropping to her stomach now and I was reminded of Troy and the cabin he hoped to build along the banks of the Au Train River.

"Okay," she said. "I'll help you."

I nodded, peeked around the corner of the shed again.

"There's one catch."

She looked at me. "What is it?"

I took a deep breath, praying this would work.

"Troy and your daughter get their happy ending first."

CHAPTER
TWENTY-TWO

I spent the rest of that afternoon in the house, waiting for Odessa and Cal and Dylan to come home, feeling like I should be doing something but having no idea what that something was.

Sara had promised she would help, and so I stood at the window, watching as she rode away with Esther in Jamie Stoddard's wagon.

Louise was on edge, and I found her standing on the porch, gazing at the road that would bring her daughter and grandson home.

"What's keeping them, I'd like to know?" she asked when I came to stand beside her, and I shook my head, a dark thought forming.

Had something happened at Henry Younts' cabin that had caused them to run away? And if so, what would Jamie Stoddard and his father do when they discovered the medicine bag was gone?

I crossed my arms, my gaze traveling down length of the lane and willed them to appear.

It would be difficult for the three of them to travel unnoticed, and still Butler had a way of disappearing when he wanted to.

I looked over at Louise. Her jaw was set as she wiped her hands on her apron.

"Where do you think they are?" I asked.

She shook her head. "I have no earthly idea, but if that fool girl doesn't hurry, she will look a mess at the dance." Then, turning to me. "What will you be wearing?"

I froze, unsure how to answer when a movement in the woods caught my attention.

"Did you see that?" I asked, and Louise squinted, shaded her face with her hand.

"I don't see anything."

I walked down the steps, shaded my face as well.

"It was just there," I said. "Between those big pine trees."

Louise sighed, untied her apron, and clomped down the steps to stand beside me. "It had better not be that grandson of mine making mischief when I've kept dinner waiting for him."

I shifted my weight in my new shoes and glanced at the cotton-wood tree again, hungry for a glimpse of Dylan, who was due home from the fields soon.

"I suspect it is the boy," Louise said. "Go and tell him I am through with his games, and he will not go to the dance even if he had a mind to."

A protest rose in my throat, and I swallowed it, knowing I would tell Cal no such thing when I found him.

"Don't dawdle," Louise ordered. "I'd tan his hide myself, but my knees won't carry me that far."

I stood for a moment, unsure if I should go and then made my way across the yard, my mind falling into the familiar steps it had taken so many times before.

ADAM

I said the word without hope of hearing anything in return and received my wish.

I listened to the birds in the trees, listened to the soft wind that seemed to always be blowing, thought of the hundreds of times his voice had kept me company and felt grief press my lungs.

I thought of Dylan and our argument, wondering if he had been right about destroying the totems, pictures of our night in the Rook Cabin floating through my mind. I remembered his face above me, his kisses falling over my neck and shoulders and felt my knees weaken.

I stopped, put my face against my arm and began to cry.

I wanted to go home, wanted to sit at a kitchen table on Friday night and play Euchre with Holly and Dave, wanted to wander the trails of Three Fires with Pam while Iris waited inside with a glass of lemonade. I wanted to walk into Huffs and see Mallard behind the bar, Shaw on his favorite stool as he complained about the hamburger he'd just eaten every bite of.

I wanted to close my eyes at night knowing my mother was happy and Adam was safe, wanted to fall asleep beside Dylan as he talked about the basketball team he was coaching, our children tucked away in the next room.

And still, in the perfect life I'd just imagined, something was missing.

I listened to a chickadee, saw it perch in the high pines that crested the hill between this place and the Rook Cabin.

I took a step, watched the bird fly away into darkness as a noise came from behind.

I spun around and saw Butler standing before me.

He took one step, then another, until he stood so close we could have touched.

"You have traveled far, Ogichidaa."

I froze even as I searched for the other two behind him.

"What does that mean?"

His eyes searched mine, and when he spoke it was with careful consideration. "You make war with those who have hurt your people, but can you make peace?"

I held his gaze, feeling the truth of his words even as my mind railed against them.

"Where's Cal?" I asked, turning again. "I saw him."

"He is home with his mother."

I shook my head. "I just came from there."

"Are you sure?" he asked, turning to walk deeper into the woods and I followed, stopping only when he did.

I felt something on my face, something cold running from my nose to my lips and realized it was blood. I put a hand up, hoping to cover it but Butler took my wrist, placed it at my side.

"Do not hide from this."

I looked down, my throat full, the blood drying against my skin.

"The medicine lives inside of you just as it does the boy."

I wanted to pull away, to run to the house but something held me in place.

"Cal said that looking at him was like staring into a mirror."

I lifted my head quickly; not sure I'd heard him right.

"Your brother is here."

I took a faltering step, turned quickly to look behind me.

"Where?" I asked, frantic now. "I can't hear him."

Butler looked to the trees above us. "It is not yet time to listen."

I stood still, unafraid for the first time.

"You know why I'm here, don't you?"

He looked at me, his eyes as still and deep as the Big Lake.

"The only thing that matters is that *you* know."

I pressed my lips together, unsure how to answer.

"Of course, I know."

"Then tell me."

I closed my eyes, took a breath.

"I want everything to go back to the way it was."

"Do you?"

I nodded; my eyes still closed. "And I want to have a wedding under that maple tree in our backyard, want to watch my children play on the swing set Dylan's going to build."

"Is that all?" he asked.

I felt a deep pulsing in my chest, felt the warm vibrations of the earth beneath my feet, the sounds of those who came before my people filling my ears like a drum.

"I need to stop Henry Younts."

"No," he said, the word cutting through mine like a knife.

"I need to save my brother and Dylan."

"No."

"I need to help Odessa, and you and Cal-"

"No!" he said sharply. "What are you looking for?"

I opened my eyes, the warmth I'd felt before covering me like a blanket.

"What have you always been looking for?"

I felt my body release, saw my father raking leaves in the backyard while I ran in the slippery piles, saw us watching our cardinals eat from the winter feeders, my crayons spread across the table in front of us as he sipped his coffee.

"Dad," I whispered. "I came to find my father."

"Yes," he said. "And who is your father?"

I saw the back of Mom's head as she drove us home from the community pool, watched as Sherry made a face in the backseat before she got out of the car. Then we were pulling into our driveway, and I saw Robert Cook in the front yard, his hand raised as we rolled to a stop.

I threw open the door, raced across the lawn and into his arms.

"Muffet," he said, pulling me close, my head buried against his shoulder, and I held him tightly, the first staggering wave of elation sweeping up my skin.

"You're here," I choked as his arms tightened around me.

"I always was," the voice replied, different than my father's.

I pulled back, unburied my face and looked into my own eyes, swollen from crying against the side of the bed, confetti pieces of a birthday card scattered at my feet.

"Where did he go?" she asked me, and I shook my head, pulled her to my chest again.

"Who are you looking for?" Butler asked, his voice like a dream.

"Her," I said, my body shaking now. "I'm looking for *her*."

He nodded, took a step backwards.

"A child of the Falling Leaves Moon will walk between this world and the next."

"What?" I asked.

"Find her, Ogichidaa."

I swallowed, my eyes rising to his and he smiled, his gaze lifting to the sky before turning and I watched him go, watched him take another step and did not follow the thing I thought I had wanted.

Instead, I stood, listening to the forest settle in for sleep, the sky a rosy hue that said dusk was near.

A moment passed, and then another as I stood alone in the woods, unsure where to go when a voice broke free, my name on their lips and I remembered that I was looking for Cal and that Louise would be angry I had taken so long.

I turned, my mind heavy as I staggered between the trees, a glimpse of the boy I'd come to find appearing in front of me.

"Cal," I cried out, and he turned, ran to me, his eyes wide with worry.

"What are you doing out here?" he said, breathless.

"I was looking for you," I said, glad he was here. "I saw you in the pine trees by the house."

He shook his head. "I came home with Ma. Gran sent Dylan and me out when you didn't come back."

"How long have I been gone?" I asked.

"Almost an hour," he said, his eyes dropping to my lips where the blood had dried against them.

"Butler was here."

The boy looked at me as though he knew something I didn't.

"He's at his cabin," he said. "Has been most of the afternoon."

"No," I said. "He was here, talking to me and then he was gone."

Cal shook his head.

"We need to get you back before Gran ties a cowbell around your neck like she's threatening to."

I wanted to laugh but let him take my hand instead, let him lead me through the trees because I didn't know what else to do.

It wasn't long before we heard Dylan calling my name.

"I found her!" Cal cried in return, and I watched as he came towards us, a look of relief in his eyes when he saw me.

Turning to Cal, he put a hand on his shoulder. "Go tell your grandmother she's all right."

Cal nodded, his eyes cutting to me before running off the way he had come.

We stood for a moment, not moving, the words we'd spoken hanging heavy between us.

"Where were you?" he asked.

"I went looking for Cal and then," I shook my head, unsure. "I must have gotten lost."

"There's blood on your face," he paused, touched my cheek. "What happened?"

I thought about Butler, feeling like the words he'd spoken were only for me.

"The medicine is alive, Dylan," I said.

He looked at me, his eyes dark with uncertainty.

"I came in from the fields and you weren't there," he stopped, his voice shaky. "It felt like the Whisper Stone all over again... and the Falls."

I went to him, and he put his arms around my back, pulled me against him.

"I'm sorry about what I said," he whispered, his chin resting on top of my head.

"Dylan,"

"If there's another path, I know you'll find it."

I tensed; unsure I'd heard him right.

"And I promise I'll follow wherever it leads."

I pulled back to look at him, knowing this type of surrender went against everything he was made of.

"Can you put that in writing?"

He put his head back, laughed into the October sky and I was reminded of the day we'd found each other again on a lonely stretch of road outside Lantern Creek.

"Ready to get back to our life?" I asked. "Our *real* life?"

He smiled. "Back to boring?"

I shook my head. "No promises, Locke."

He leaned closer, his lips seeking mine.

"Good."

TWENTY-THREE

Cal was sitting at the kitchen table, eating a small meal from the leftover beans and stew the others had eaten for lunch, his ma at the kitchen basin. He'd caught her looking over her shoulder at him, caught her watching the backyard for signs of Dylan and Justine.

Or someone else.

It was almost time for the dance, and his gran had decided to let him go even though she said he had been very foolish the day before and he knew deep in his heart that she had been worried.

And that had surprised him.

Voices at the door made him look up quickly.

He knew Dylan was anxious when he came in from the fields to find Justine gone, knew he was holding his fear inside because Cal recognized the same look in Butler's eyes when his ma had decided to walk to town one afternoon in early July.

Word came to the farm shortly after that a mother bear and two cubs had been spotted by the river and Cal remembered Butler watching the woods as they worked to repair the shed in the backyard.

His smile had been tight, his movements those of a man ready to run at any moment and when his ma returned a few hours later, he'd gone to her, and they had talked quietly for a long time.

He'd seen the same look in Dylan's eyes as they began their search and knew it was because he loved Justine and that things had been left unsaid between them.

Now, as they entered the house, he could see that everything was all right, and it made him happy to know she wouldn't be alone when they stole away into the night.

Cal felt his mind wander as he sat eating his food, felt fear creep up and touch his neck as his gran, true to her word, threatened to give Justine a cowbell. Then she was bustling her off to the bedroom, muttering all the while how an ordinary dress wouldn't do for a night like tonight.

Cal sat in the chair, watching while Dylan changed into pair of trousers his grandpa had worn. Paired with a white cotton shirt and cloth jacket, he just passed Gran's inspection.

Soon Justine emerged in a green gingham dress that made her eyes change color, her hair loosely braided around her face, and Cal thought he had never seen her look so pretty.

Johnny stood waiting, dressed in a black button-down shirt and vest, his hair slicked down over his forehead as he called for the others to hurry up and get in the wagon.

Cal saw his ma, pretty in her best pink dress, nod to him and he stood, took a step when the June bugs began to buzz in his ears again

DON'T GO WITH THEM

Cal felt his shoulders tense as he fought to keep his face still. WHY?

TAKE THE LONG WAY THROUGH THE VALLEY

Cal stood, watching the others as they made their way towards the door, unsure what to do when his ma turned to him.

"Son?" she asked, her dark eyes holding his and he opened his mouth as his gran came into view, the feathers on her bonnet waving as she fought to catch her breath.

"LeRoy Burks and Timothy Quinn want to meet at the cross-roads," he said quickly. "I can walk with them from there."

"Nonsense," his gran shook her head. "You're just on the mend and I'll not have you rambling around the countryside with that awful Burks boy."

His eyes went to his ma again and she nodded.

"I will allow it," she said, her back straight as a ramrod and he was reminded of what she had done to Preacher Younts in his cabin that morning.

"Odessa," his gran gasped, the feathers in her bonnet shaking wildly now. "I have already told him he may not go."

He watched his ma turn towards his gran and knew she wasn't afraid anymore.

"He is my child and will do as I say."

Cal watched his gran's mouth open, saw Dylan and Justine cast nervous glances at each other.

"How *dare* you," his gran hissed. "You brazen little,"

"Go, Son," his ma interrupted. "We will see you at the dance."

Cal smiled, his heart set free even as his gran untied her bonnet and slammed it down on the table.

"I feel a headache coming on," she frowned, her eyes on her daughter. "And will have to miss the dance on account of it."

"What a shame," Odessa said. "Penelope Karsten will surely take note of your absence."

Cal watched his gran get red in the face, watched her little hands ball up into fists.

"Go fetch my bottle," she spat, and her daughter tilted her head, a small smile on her lips.

"Get it yourself."

Cal watched his grandmother take a step backwards, her mouth a perfect O as his ma nodded to her brother.

One glance at Louise and Johnny stood, unsure what to do.

"Ma?" he asked, and she opened her mouth, unable to speak.

"Come, Johnny," his ma said, and he looked between his mother and sister one last time before following her out the door.

Cal stood, watching as the others left, a heaviness settling over the house as his gran muttered under her breath about the ruin the family was coming to.

"Go on, then," she muttered at him. "Do as you're told but do not expect to find shelter under my roof when you come back."

He stood, the momentum of her words making him dizzy as she sank into her chair.

It wasn't long before he heard her snoring and so he crept up to look at her.

His gran's head had fallen to the side, her mouth open as a small rivulet of spittle ran down her chin.

Repulsed, he wondered why he had never taken a moment to look at her, to see her for what she really was, and it made him wonder how she had come to be this way.

He stood behind her, marveling at how things would have been different without the bottle, and knew it was the reason behind the tight knot of fear that seemed to live inside his stomach.

"Goodbye, Gran," he whispered, and she stirred.

"I cannot abide it, Seth," she said, her voice hoarse and Cal stood taller, wondering if she knew what she was saying or if the laudanum had made her delirious.

"It is the drink talking, I am certain of it."

Cal looked closely now and saw that half the bottle was gone.

"Johnny does not remember and that is a blessing."

Cal touched her shoulder, wanting to calm her and at the same time wanting her to continue and felt a strange sensation course through his arms and legs. The next instant he saw the woods, saw the lanterns being lit as a young boy and man he assumed was his father stood on the edge of a deep ravine.

Cal looked behind him, hoping to see the house he'd always known when the man began to speak.

"Do you see the deer, Johnny?" he said, his tone harsh and the boy nodded, his small hands reaching for his father as he pushed him away.

"Stand still," he barked, "I am going to shoot it."

At once the boy let out a sharp cry and his father turned, a look of loathing on his face and Cal knew he had been drinking, recognized the vacant look he had seen in his gran's eyes many times before.

Taking hold of the gun, Johnny tried to pull just as his father jerked it away, the butt end catching him in the face as he tumbled backwards.

The man yelled, then jumped into the gully to chase after his son.

Cal looked behind him again, saw nothing but the darkened woods and took a step down the side of the valley, then another until he was standing beside them, the boy crumpled into a ball as the man he knew now to be his grandfather knelt beside him.

Johnny was still, his father shivering as he turned him over. A rock smeared with something red lay just beneath the back of his head and the man gave a low cry.

Cal watched Seth rise, watched him wipe his face with his hand before stumbling backwards, his boot catching on a root that sent him sprawling in the leaves. Then he was staggering to his feet, scrambling back up the side of ravine and out of sight.

Cal felt his heart freeze, the whispered mystery of what had happened to his uncle a terrible reality now.

Trembling, he turned and ran up out of the valley and through the woods until he felt his arms and legs become heavy again, his vision clear as the house came into focus around him.

His gran lay sleeping, her breath labored, and Cal understood for the first time what the bottle in her hand had buried.

HURRY

He swiped at his face and the unshed tears that rested there and ran out the door.

TWENTY-FOUR

The Karsten Farm, located on the top of a hill and crowned with a thousand flickering lights, was more beautiful than I had ever imagined. I drew a deep breath, looked over at Dylan as he rode beside me in the wagon and could only guess at what he was feeling.

I put my arm through his, squeezed tightly while leaning into his shoulder as we bounced along, Johnny and Odessa on the high seat in front of us and he looked down on me, smiled in a way that said he couldn't believe what was happening.

"This doesn't seem real," he paused, his hand closing over mine. "But it is."

I nodded, the scene back at the house temporarily forgotten as we took in the view. And still, Odessa's sudden show of strength and Cal's desire to walk with the schoolyard bully I'd heard him complain about made me uneasy.

"Are you okay?" Dylan whispered and I smiled, loving, and hating how he could read my mood as I glanced up at Odessa.

"Yes," I said, watching as My grandmother sat like a statue, looking neither left nor right as we rolled to a stop in front of a large barn that sat behind an impressive house.

Music drifted on the wind as people in bright clothing strolled by in the climbing moonlight. I closed my eyes, breathed deeply, imagining that Dylan and I were where we were supposed to be, living the life we'd always meant to.

Moments later a group of people gathered around the wagon to greet us, all blond and beautiful and in some way resembling the man sitting beside me, who had suddenly gone very still.

"Dylan?" I asked, laying a hand on his forearm and he tensed.

"I'm okay," he assured me. "It's not every day a guy gets to meet all his grandparents at once."

I watched Odessa's face melt into a lovely smile as Andrew approached, offering her his hand as she stepped down from the wagon.

Moments later he was greeting Dylan, a stunned look on his face.

"I see why Justine was frightened when we met," he smiled, clapped him on the back. "Are you sure you're not related to us?"

Dylan shook his head, rattled off the lie about being from downstate and it seemed to satisfy Andrew as I moved closer, touched his arm.

"Where's Sara?"

He shook his head, glanced back at the other wagons that were pulling up behind ours.

"She's riding with Esther, although I thought they would be here by now."

I tried not to worry, nodded instead while gathering my skirt and following Odessa and Johnny towards the barn.

Then we were inside, and I was surrounded by the sights and sounds and smells of the most beautiful scene I'd ever witnessed.

The barn was large, the ceiling and low beams hung with evergreen garlands and colorful leaves, silver ribbon sparkling in the lantern light.

Hay bales had been drawn to the sides and were filled with people, their laughter rising above the cheerful tempo of a jig. I drew closer, saw that two fiddlers had taken up residence in a far corner, their high notes complimenting the accordion player who stood between them.

I squeezed Dylan's hand, the wild hope that we could enjoy a portion of what his family had so carefully prepared taking root in my heart.

Movement caught my eye. People were twirling, their patterns reminding me of a square dance my mother had forced me to participate in during a particularly low point in my adolescence.

And still I was swept away, forgetting for the moment what I had come here to do.

Then we were moving towards the food, watching as cups of punch were poured and pieces of pie served. I took a china plate and Dylan did the same, hardly believing we could do something as simple as enjoy a party when the weight of the world hung in the balance.

"I don't believe we have met," a voice to my right caught my attention and I turned, looked into the eyes of a woman who could have been Melinda Locke's sister.

I opened my mouth, prepared for my typical inadequacy when a younger woman came to stand beside her.

"I'm Penelope Karsten," the older woman said, resplendent in a white dress that seemed to float away in an otherworldly mass of pleats and bustles. "And this is my daughter, Abigail."

I bowed my head, watched Dylan do the same.

"I believe you already know my son, Andrew."

"Yes," I nodded, caught off balance by her presence and understood why Louise so desperately wanted to impress her.

Then she began to speak, her voice rising with excitement as she asked about our travels and how Dylan had found me at the Cook Homestead.

"Please let us know if there is anything we can do for you,"

Abigail said, her blue eyes dancing and I smiled, forever grateful that her friendship with Odessa had brought Dylan into my life.

"Thank you," I replied, my eyes wandering from her lavender dress to the door as I scanned the room for Sara and Cal and Henry Younts.

Then Dylan was squeezing my hand, and Penelope was nodding to us, encouraging us to go and enjoy the music because a waltz was about to begin. I smiled, bowed my head again as I watched other couples move to the middle of the floor.

Odessa was there, dancing with an awkward Johnny while a woman began to sing about the Red River Valley, her voice spilling into the open fields. I imagined Cal walking the darkened road, imagined his head lifting towards the crown of the hill and hoped the music would lead him to us.

Then I was in Dylan's arms, his hand at my waist as we moved in slow circles, the whole world dissolving into bliss and I wanted to stay, wanted to change my mind and never return to the Whisper Stone if it meant even a piece of this world would live inside of me forever.

"What are you thinking?" Dylan asked, his face close to mine and I smiled.

"The same thing you are."

He pulled back, his eyes crinkling at the corners. "Wanna stay?"

"Don't tempt me."

His hands tightened on my waist.

"Dylan,"

"I'd do it," he said, his voice low. "If it meant we could be together."

I felt my throat tighten as the music drifted off into the moonlight, the singer bowing to enthusiastic applause and waited, wishing for another song to follow.

And then another.

A hand on my elbow, light yet insistent and I turned to see Sara Bennett beside me.

One glance at Dylan and her eyes went wide, the realization that I had honestly mistaken him for Andrew showing on her face.

"Pleased to meet you," she stammered, undone by the similarity and I took a step to the side, motioned for Dylan to follow us.

"Esther won't tell me anything," she whispered.

"Why?" I repeated, following her from the center of the floor to the hay bales, where we lingered in the shadows of the lantern light.

"I don't know," she said, her face twisted, her movements agitated.

"Do you think they plan on sneaking away?" I asked, turning to Dylan.

He pressed his lips together, shook his head. "We need to find out. Where are they?"

I felt my heart speed up, my eyes searching the barn as Andrew appeared at Sara's side.

"There you are," he teased, his mood light. "I've been saving a dance."

"Has Esther come inside yet?" she asked, and he shook his head, caught off guard.

"Jonas Younts helped her out of the wagon. They were outside talking."

"*Were?*" she asked, and I felt my blood run cold. "Where are they now?"

Andrews's smile faded as he turned to look behind him and I felt my skin prickle, the enchanted feeling of a moment before gone.

"Why does it matter?" Andrew asked, his arm around Sara's waist and I looked into her eyes, remembering what I'd asked her to do as we scanned the crowd.

Moments later I was pushing through the people, heading towards the door as Esther entered, sublime in a blue velvet dress, her hair hanging in thick curls over her shoulders as Jamie Stoddard came to stand beside her.

I felt Dylan put a hand on my arm, stopping me. His face hardened, perhaps remembering the moment they had stood on the break wall at Salmon Fest.

"Stoddard," he whispered, shaken by the sight and I pulled him forward, anxious to talk to the woman who had been so kind to me that afternoon when a flash of pink caught my eye.

Odessa- moving from some far corner, her gaze shifting to the doorway as Henry Younts stepped into the barn behind his son.

I felt Dylan's grip tighten and knew it took every ounce of his strength to remain where he was.

One glance at my grandmother and the preacher was moving towards her, a look in his eye that said he would take what he wanted.

I felt the room shift, felt the laughter fade away as people turned to watch.

"Dess," he said, standing in front of her now, his breath heavy in the quiet room.

"Mr. Younts," she replied, her tone dismissive. The preacher's face flushed, and I knew he was thinking of the embarrassment she had caused him.

"You said you would come to the dance with me, and I expect you to make good on that promise."

Penelope Karsten put a hand over her mouth, leaned towards a man I assumed was her husband as Abigail stood frozen at their side.

"I am here, Mr. Younts," Odessa said, her voice seeming to rise to the rafters. "But I have no intention of sharing a dance with you tonight nor any time after."

Henry Younts swallowed, his Adam's apple bobbing and for a fleeting moment I felt pity.

"Surely you knew..." he whispered, and I thought of the man

who had argued with his wife before she died, the man who now stood humiliated by the woman he hoped would take her place.

"I know nothing aside from the workings of my own heart."

"Dess," he said, hopeless now.

"And because of that I must ask you leave."

The preacher's face twisted, and I heard the muffled gasps of the beautiful people in the colorful clothes as he took hold of her arm.

"Listen here,"

At once the sounds in the room went muffled, the hum of white noise building in my ears as rage roiled inside of me, a picture of the little girl at the community pool appearing before my eyes.

Find her...

And the father she adored, walking into the woods behind Ocqueoc Falls to face her enemy for her.

I stepped forward, my hands gnarled hooks as I took hold of his shoulder.

"Get away from her."

He turned to me, his eyes wide and unbelieving as he fought to shake my grip.

"Justine," Odessa said, more a statement than a question, and then Henry Younts was laughing, shaking his head as he looked to Dylan, who stood behind me.

"You must be the one who ran off instead of tending to the boy" he said, and Dylan tensed. "You gonna do something about her?"

"Not on your life," Dylan replied, his words calculated as we stood in an awful tableau, Henry Younts' eyes darkening to the black pitch I remembered as he withered under my grip, swaying for a moment before crashing forward in a fit of fury.

The beautiful creatures in the bright dresses scattered, and I heard their screams, saw men reaching for their guns as I ducked beneath the preacher's arm.

Off balance now, he teetered on his feet, and I rushed towards him, burying my fist in his gut.

A low groan as he stumbled sideways, his hands splayed in front of him and at once I was surrounded, Odessa lost in the mass of panicked faces as Dylan took hold of my arm.

"They know," he said, and I touched my lip, felt blood on my fingertips.

"It's the shaman," someone shouted. "He's done something to her."

I turned again, saw them whispering behind gloved hands, my heart burning as I took a step back.

Another step and I was spinning, looking for Esther and Jamie in the place I had last seen them, but the doorway was empty.

GET OUT

I heard his voice, felt my knees weaken beneath me.

"Let's go," Dylan whispered, pulling me backwards, shoving people aside and I took his hand, my pulse pounding in my ears as I ran.

CHAPTER
TWENTY-FIVE

Cal waded through the darkness like he was back in the river, cautiously and with fear clinging to him like a second skin.

The boy who looked like a mirror had told him to take the long way to the Karsten Farm and he wasn't sure why. He only knew that his ma had gone ahead, and Gran had stayed behind and that Butler had told him the time for their great journey was at hand.

High above he heard an owl, listened as its wings beat the air and tried to remember the path he had taken before.

He'd spent some time with Andrew Karsten before Butler had come to the farm, had enjoyed his company so much he'd hoped his ma would take a shine to him.

But she only thought of him as a friend, and then Sara Bennett had moved in with the Ebersoles and that had been the end of that.

Still, there were enough sun-filled afternoons spent between his place and the Karsten Farm that he felt sure he could find the way even in the darkest of nights.

Making his way past the edge of the field where he had first found Justine, Cal wondered if his gran would make good on her promise to turn them out. Then he thought about Ana again, her blond braids floating in the water of the deadfall and didn't care what she did to them.

That life was over.

And he was ready for a new one.

GO TO THE PLACE WHERE YOU SAW THE WOLF

Cal heard it, not questioning now, just listening to the voice as though it had always been there.

The summer before last he had been with Andrew in a deep valley only about a mile from the farm. The evening was still, the sky a sharp orange when they saw a wolf watching them in the fading light.

Andrew had taken out his rifle, told Cal to stay back because where one wolf was, there were sure to be more lurking in the darkness.

Cal remembered his mouth being dry, remembered thinking about what would happen if there were more than one when Andrew lowered his gun.

"He's alone," he'd said. "He must be old and sick to be left behind like that."

They stood watching it, aware that they were putting themselves in danger. But the wolf just stood, it's yellow eyes weary before lowering its head and jogging off into the woods.

"Why didn't you shoot it?" he asked, and Andrew shook his head.

"Maybe I was hoping he'd find his pack again."

Cal remembered thinking about it later as he lay in bed, a long howl piercing the stillness of the winter night. He pictured the animal alone in some forgotten corner of the forest and wished for a moment that Andrew had shot it.

He picked his way through the darkness, the memory still fresh in his mind when he came to the valley.

WHAT DO I DO?

He waited for the response, his breath in his ears.

WAIT

He sat down on a bed of pine needles, rested his chin on top of his knees as the sound of laughter drifted over the hills.

Minutes blended from one to the next when a slight rustling caught his attention. He listened as they drew closer, then scooted back towards a thicket where he wouldn't be seen.

Moments later Henry Younts came into view, his large form visible in the moonlight, followed by Abraham Ebersole's brother.

"We need to do it tonight," the latter said, his voice agitated.

"Now ain't the time, Ethan," the preacher grumbled, turning slowly and for an instant Cal was afraid he had seen him.

"Abraham is planning to move the gold before he takes Esther west," Ethan insisted. "It'll be too late."

"That ain't my concern," Preacher replied. "And besides... I need to speak with Dess."

Ethan laughed, startling the forest.

"Seems she got the better of you this morning."

He heard the preacher mumble something, his voice catching on the wind.

"She was fussed up is all. Got a soft spot for that boy of hers."

"She's got a soft spot for someone else, too," a slight pause. "Unless you can turn her head in your direction."

Cal waited for the preacher's response.

"Think, Henry," Ethan continued. "She's had nothing all her life and would likely do anything for a fine home and some fancy clothes. Why, she might even marry a man she doesn't love."

Cal sucked in his breath.

"She ain't that way," Preacher said. "And that shaman's been by her side since spring."

Ethan laughed again, the sound tapering into something that made Cal sick to his stomach. "Then we'll just have to take care of that, won't we?"

Cal felt a rough, senseless terror fill his veins, one that would have sent him headlong into the valley had the boy's voice not stopped him.

STAY STILL

"I ain't about to do something stupid," Preacher said, moving ahead a bit, the lights of the barn burning through the trees as though he didn't want to be there in the darkness. "I just need to talk to Dess."

"Suit yourself," Ethan said. "But soon enough you'll come around to my way of thinking."

A mumble from the preacher, followed by crunching footsteps as they wound their way out of the valley, the sound of fiddle music on the wind.

Cal sat still for a long while after they left, his heart beating so quickly he could feel it in his ears.

Not only was Preacher planning to rob Abraham, he was also going to the dance to confront his ma and if she did something like she had at the cabin...

We'll just have to take care of that, won't we?

Cal stood up, one hand braced against a tree and took a faltering step.

He knew he had to walk, knew he had to tell someone what was going to happen so they could stop it.

One step turned into another until soon he was running, faster and faster until it seemed his feet weren't touching the ground at all, the moonlight leading the way as he came up the side of the hill.

The Karsten barn stood at the top of it, blazing like a ship he'd seen in a picture once and he wanted to run to his ma, to tell her everything he'd heard when a figure passed in front of him.

He turned; his balance lost as Justine slid to a halt.

"Cal," she breathed as Dylan came rushing up behind. "What are you doing out here?"

He shook his head, unable to believe she was here.

"I heard something bad," he said. "I need to tell Ma."

She shook her head. "You can't go up there."

"I have to,"

"Tell me," she dropped to her knees, took his shoulders in her hands. "What did you hear?"

He bit his lip, unsure of what he should do when he remembered the boy, remembered that this was his sister.

"Preacher Younts and Ethan are going to steal Abraham's gold tonight," he paused, his voice peppered with fear. "They're going to hurt Butler."

They exchanged glances and he felt his anxiety rise.

"Preacher said he needed to talk to Ma, but I don't know why."

"Cal,"

"Did he say something to her?"

He felt Justine's hand tighten on his shoulder.

"You need to go home."

"*No.*"

"And you need to stay there."

He shook his head, pulled away. "Your *brother* told me to come here."

She pulled back, her face searching his.

"My brother?"

Cal stood still, a feeling of guilt washing over him.

"He told me to take the long way to the farm and to listen to what they said, and I believe he's trying to help us... trying to help *you*,"

She looked down, her face still in the moonlight. "He is."

He covered her hand with his own, relief sweeping his skin.

"I'm not crazy, then?"

She laughed lightly, shook her head.

"No more than I am."

Cal stood still, unsure what to say when she stood again. Turning to Dylan, she took his hand in hers.

"Something bad is going to happen at the Ebersole farm

tonight," he said. "We came here to stop it but... I don't think we can."

"*What?*"

"You need to go home and stay with your mother."

He thought again of Butler, thought of their plan to travel to the shores of the Gichigami.

"I can't," he whispered. "We *can't*,"

"You're running away, aren't you?" Justine asked.

He swallowed, the feeling of guilt making him weak.

"We won't try and stop you," she said.

Dylan moved, put a hand to the back of his head as though he wanted to say something but couldn't.

"You're free to go."

Cal felt his breath catch, the picture of the boy who looked like a mirror flickering before him until he didn't know what was real.

"Where did you come from?" he asked, having no idea why he had said it.

"Cal,"

"There weren't any bandits, were there?"

She stood still; her hands clasped in front of her.

"Butler said the medicine lives inside of me."

She looked at him, then at Dylan again.

"It lives inside of you, too, doesn't it?"

He felt her silence like a heartbeat.

"Does it scare you?" he whispered.

She hugged herself in the chilly air, nodded so quickly he almost missed it.

"Does it ever get better?"

"Sometimes," she whispered, and then Dylan came up behind her, put his hands on her shoulders.

"We need to go," he said, looking up at the stars as they hung over the pine trees.

"Sometimes when I'm lost, I follow the drinking gourd," Cal said.

"The drinking gourd?" she asked, looking up.

"It's right there," he said, his finger tracing the sky. "And if you draw a line, you can find the North Star."

Voices carried from the barn behind them, followed by the sounds of wagons rattling down the hill.

"Gran says it never changes," he said, thinking of her. "She says it's always the same."

"Where will it take us?"

He thought for a minute, his mind wandering to the yellow trees he had lingered beneath that morning.

"To the Ebersole's."

"And after that?" she asked.

He took a breath, saw a rock rise above a field of snow.

"The Whisper Stone."

TWENTY-SIX

I t seemed like we'd been walking forever, the North Star just above when our feet found a dust-covered lane. I looked down at the shoes Esther had given me that morning, wondering if this was the same place where I'd jumped from Jamie's Stoddard's truck.

I thought about Henry Younts and his red pickup, a gun pointed at my head as we bounced along the road that led to Back Forty Farm and tried to quiet my mind.

Make the path, Muffet...

But there wasn't one, only a muddled maze that led to a world I wouldn't recognize when I returned to it.

"Why didn't you ask Cal about the medicine bag?" Dylan asked, and I stopped, my heart in my throat.

"That's not the answer."

"Then what is?"

I stopped, looked at him and knew he wasn't angry but simply seeking the answers that had always made him feel safe.

"Maybe we can get to the Whisper Stone."

"No," I shook my head. "We're not done here yet."

"It's too late to save Esther... and Jamie."

"You don't know that."

"J," he said, his promise to follow me hanging between us before he paused, looked up again. "Okay... just tell me what to do."

I turned, the road reaching towards a dark bend I seemed to remember when a gunshot split the air in two.

I felt Dylan grab my arm, felt him pull me towards the side of the road even as we took off at a scrambling run.

It didn't take long to reach the lonely farmhouse, and I came up short when I saw it, the tree that caught fire but never burned reaching a gnarled hand towards the dusky moon.

"Justine," Dylan whispered, crouching behind a tree as figures moved in the barnyard, a light burning in the stall of Abraham's favorite gelding. "*Get down.*"

I did as he said, heard a groan as Jamie Stoddard knelt in the dirt, Esther Ebersole dead in his arms.

I felt my breath seize up, thinking of the white handkerchief peppered with blood as Jamie rocked on his knees, a series of low sobs turning my stomach.

Then Henry Younts shuffled towards his son, pulled him up by the scruff of the neck.

"Git up, boy!" I heard him growl. "We need to cover our tracks."

Jamie didn't respond, just stood in place and I remembered how he had looked while sitting beneath the oak tree that afternoon, knew how his heart must be breaking and turning and falling in on top of itself.

"Git your wits about you," his father said. "And set Orion loose."

"Pa," Jamie said, his voice barely a whisper. "I can't..."

"They'll think the killer rode out on him."

"I can't think," Jamie said, his voice rising now. "I can't *breathe.*"

"You should've thought of that before you took up with a

married woman," Henry Younts growled. "All I was trying to do was make a better life for us and here you were, screwing her in the stables."

'No, Pa," Jamie said, his voice breaking. "I loved her. And she loved me."

"No one loves you, boy," his father said. "Especially not a woman like her."

"You're wrong," his son said, pacing in a small circle now, pausing to kneel beside Esther again and I knew he must be out of his mind even as his voice seemed steady. "And I'm going to find a way for us to be together."

"Listen, here,"

"Johnny Cook said that shaman brought a barn cat back to life."

"We gotta make ourselves *scarce,* boy."

"If we could find him, or that medicine bag,"

"She's gone!" his father bellowed, "And you'd best get used to it."

Another silence, another glance at Esther and I knew Jamie was considering how he could join her as he touched the revolver on his belt.

"You should take your own advice, Pa."

I tensed, unsure what would happen next when a movement from an upper window caught my eye. A white nightdress-blinding in the moonlight and Ethan Ebersole saw it, gave a low cry from the locust tree he'd been hiding in.

"She's getting away," Henry shouted as Ethan jumped from the tree, his staggered footsteps taking him to Esther.

"No," he said, dazed as Henry grabbed him by the collar of his shirt.

"Git her!" he ordered, and Ethan turned quickly, took off running.

"What's she doing?" Dylan said. "I thought she knew about us."

193

"She does," I held a hand up, watching as Jamie gathered Esther carefully in his arms and carried her into the house. "What was the name of that horse?"

He shook his head. "Orion, I think. *Why?*"

"Where would his home be?"

He turned, the flickering light of the lantern drawing our eyes to his stall.

"We need to go there."

His jaw tightened and I knew he wasn't pleased about walking into a place where we could easily be trapped.

The next moment I heard a gate swing open, heard a neighing sound as a beautiful horse with four white socks walked into the center alley. He lifted his head, nostrils flared, still spooked by the gunshots and the smell of blood.

Jamie grabbed his bridle, slapped his side and the horse reared up on his hind legs only to come down hard a moment later. Then he was tearing towards us, and we gripped the trunk of the tree, watching as he sped past and disappeared into the night.

"We need to go," I said, standing up slowly, watching as Jamie and his father made their way around the back of the house.

"Okay," he whispered, "But stay close to me."

I nodded, my senses on high alert as I followed him across the barnyard, stopping once to listen for any sound other than the rustling of long dead leaves.

Once inside the alley, I watched as one by one the other horses stuck their heads out of the stalls and I prayed they would stay silent, prayed we could find what we were looking for as we approached Orion's stall.

Dylan stood by the door, scoping out the alley as I crept inside.

"Hurry," he instructed, looking one way, and then the other as I turned in a slow circle. There was hay in the corner, various tack on the wall and one window that someone had left halfway open.

The next moment Dylan was inside the stall, dragging me

down beside him as he pulled the gate inward, creating a darkened corner we slunk down into.

I looked at him and he put a finger to his lips. Heavy footfalls sounded in the alley, pausing right outside the stall.

Then they passed by, the heavy clomp of boots entering the next stall over.

I didn't dare breathe, my hand clutching Dylan's as the footsteps made a slow circle of the stall. I heard fabric brush against itself, heard the slight jingle of tack being touched and wondered what he was doing and if we could ever escape this place with our lives.

"Been a long spell, Becky" he said, and even though his voice was a soft as I'd ever heard it, I recognized the speaker as Henry Younts.

Silence, and for a moment I thought he might have been sitting, looking up at the ceiling and the low wall that separated us when I heard him moving again, his footfalls stiff on the wooden floor.

"Forgive me," he muttered, and I watched, my knuckles white as his long shadow fell across the doorway.

We saw it turn, watched him pause just on the other side of our gate.

I sat crouching in a silence so potent it might have been alive, expecting to see black eyes staring at me over the top of the gate before I finally heard him retreat down the alley and out of the barn.

I felt Dylan's body release, felt his hand loosen in mine as I collapsed against him, my breathing labored from holding it for so long.

"We need to get out of here," he whispered, and I glanced behind, dread crippling me and if I could just stand up, could just gather my senses-

LOOK UP!

I heard the voice and jumped to my feet.

"J," Dylan gripped my arm, his face slashed with panic. "Don't-"

I went to the lantern, took it off the wall.

"There," I pointed, the light leaping from plank to plank as a picture suddenly materialized just above the open window.

A cluster of stars, painted with a careful hand.

"It's Orion," Dylan breathed, turning to me. "Did Esther,"

"Yes," I whispered while climbing on top of a small stool that stood next to the trough.

A small shelf cupped the corner, forgotten with age and dusted with cobwebs and I touched it, felt something cool beneath my fingertips.

"There's something up here," I said, and Dylan took the lantern, held it high so I could see.

A glint caught my eye and I reached out, took it in my hand while jumping down from the stool.

"What is it?" Dylan asked, and we bent closer, a golden ring shining in the middle of my palm.

I've spent enough time looking for things that will never return to me...

I felt the silence gather around me again, a living, breathing thing that seemed to speak of what I'd been looking for.

"Henry Younts' wife died after being thrown from a horse," I said. "He couldn't find her wedding ring."

"Is this it?" he asked, touching it with a careful finger.

I nodded. "She must have taken it off before she went riding. No one knew it was there."

"Can you," Dylan began, his hand on my arm. "Can you *see* what happened?"

I swallowed, knowing we should get out of the stall but feeling like I needed to understand this one thing more than anything else in my life.

I closed my eyes and stilled my mind, tried to feel the cold metal of the ring I held and the connection it had to this place.

I saw a woman, her brown hair bunched in a bun at the nape of her neck as she pulled on her riding gloves. Then she was peeling them off, standing on the stool and placing the ring safely on the high shelf. I watched Orion stir, watched his nostrils flare as he kicked out with his back leg, knocking her into the wall.

I saw her fall, heard a hollow sound as her head hit the trough, her body still as the horse reared up and ran from the stall.

Moments later two men appeared in the doorway, arguing about which horse had been tacked up as a young Abraham Ebersole appeared behind them, his face drawn up in horror.

"Why was she in here?" he shouted. "I am the only one who can ride him and he does not like the smell of a woman."

"She switched 'em, sir," one of the men said while looking fearfully at the other. "We had Hector all ready to go."

"That will do us no good when Henry finds out," Abraham raged. "I've spent too much money on that horse to have him shot by an angry husband."

The men looked at each other, unsure of what to say.

"We must tell him it was Hector. I was going to sell him, and this will save me the trouble."

The others nodded, satisfied with the plan as they bent to pick up Henry's wife, the dark events that had triggered a transformation in her husband set in motion and I blinked, the stall materializing before me.

"What did you see?" Dylan asked softly, and I squeezed his hand, undone by what I had seen.

"She was putting her ring on that shelf when Orion kicked the stool out from under her," I said. "Henry Younts thinks she was angry at him, thinks she took it off on purpose."

Dylan frowned, his eyes darkening. "Do you think he blames himself?"

THEY LIVE WHERE HENRY YOUNTS DIED...

I nodded, the path suddenly clear.

The next moment I was pulling tack off the wall while trying to decide which of the Ebersole's remaining horses would get us to the Whisper Stone the fastest.

"What are you doing?" Dylan asked, one hand on my arm as if to stop me even as his eyes told me he knew exactly what to do.

"We need to tell him the truth," I said, halfway out of the stall now.

He shook his head. "How?"

I took the ring out, held it to the light.

"With this."

CHAPTER
TWENTY-SEVEN

C al saw the windows of his home shining in the darkness, his time in the woods with Dylan and Justine running like a rabbit through his mind. He'd always felt that she came from another place, but now that she had spoken the words to him, he felt closer to her, a part of himself he didn't know existed opening to the possibility that he could help her as well.

Follow the drinking gourd...

He'd shown her the way to go, then sat for a bit in the valley after they had vanished, thinking about what she'd said.

Now she would get back to the place she'd come from, and maybe if she lived a long and happy life with Dylan it would help erase a bit of the ache left in his heart.

He heard an owl in the distance again, felt the presence of death press close on all sides and watched the door of the house open, his mother's form blocking the light.

"Ma!" he cried, running towards her now and she met him on the bottom step, her best pink dress replaced by the worn gingham she used for everyday work as she pulled him into a hug.

"Sakes alive," she breathed, holding him close. "I thought you would never get here."

He felt bad for making her worry, especially on the night they were supposed to run away, and he wondered where Butler was and if he had spoken to her.

"I saw Dylan and Justine," he said. "And Preacher and Ethan."

Her body tightened, her hands gripping his shoulders in a way that told him he'd surprised her.

"Where were you?"

He wondered if he should tell her the truth and if she would be mad at him for lying to her about meeting LeRoy Burks.

"I was hiding in the valley, where I saw that wolf with Andrew. Preacher and Ethan came out of the woods and said they were going to take Abraham's gold."

She was still, listening intently.

"They were going to hurt Butler," he said. "Preacher was mad you liked him an-"

"I know, Son," she said. "The shaman has shown me everything that lives inside of his heart."

Cal looked down, wondering what was next.

As if reading his mind, his mother touched his shoulder. "We must hurry. Butler will be waiting for us by the large cedar that grows on the edge of the Falls."

Cal nodded, his heart skipping a beat as he thought about what was going to happen, hoping they wouldn't keep him waiting too long.

His ma moved up the steps again, wanting him to follow and he stood still, unable to understand why he didn't want to go inside the house again.

"I talked to Justine, Ma," he said, and she turned, the light from the house forming a silhouette behind her. "She has the medicine inside of her, too."

She turned, came slowly back down the steps, the sound of the owl carrying through the trees again.

"Cal-"

"She's like us, Ma."

She closed her eyes, her shoulders straight.

"She said I needed to come home," he paused. "It was almost like she knew what was going to happen tonight."

His mother took a breath.

"I think she does, Son," she said. "I think she's always known."

He looked up at her, knew that Butler had told her things during their night together in Preacher's cabin that would make sense when they had put this place behind them.

She moved up the steps again, turned back to look at him. "Are you ready?"

He thought about the small bag he had packed, tucked away behind his bed in the loft and knew he had to go inside to get it.

Nodding, he rushed past his mother, careful not to disturb his gran, who was still sleeping in her chair. Moving quickly now, he scampered up the ladder he'd been climbing for the past eight years, a knot of sadness tightening in his stomach.

He knew his uncle would be at the tavern, knew he could get up and back down without being seen and so he grabbed the satchel, scrambled down the ladder and saw his ma on the porch, her own bag in her hand.

"Ma-" he came up behind her, breathless when he saw a man standing in the moonlight.

A man he knew.

"Jonas," he said, his voice weak, not understanding why he would come here in the middle of the night.

His mother reached out, pulled him close to her and Cal saw why when he held up his hands.

"She's dead," he said, his voice flat, blood staining the front of his shirt.

"Jonas," his ma said softly. "Who?"

He came forward a step, stopped. "Esther."

His ma gasped, shook her head. "What happened? Was it the sickness-"

"No," he cut her off. "It was me. I killed her."

His mother's hands tightened around him.

"I don't believe it."

Jonas smiled; his face ghoulish in the moonlight. "If I hadn't wanted her so badly, hadn't been so scared she was going to go away I wouldn't have asked to meet her tonight."

"Jonas-"

"And her husband would have been none the wiser and then maybe... in time we could have been together."

Cal saw his mother pull away as she took a step towards the man.

"I am so sorry."

Jonas smiled again. "No, you're not."

Cal tensed, looked up at his ma.

"If you cared, you wouldn't be running off with that medicine bag when you know it's the only way to bring her back."

She shook her head.

"Yes," he shook a finger at her. "Johnny said that barn cat was good as new, and I know Butler has some tricks up his sleeve."

"No!"

"I ain't gonna ask again, Dess," he said, his voice lowering. "Not nicely, anyways."

Cal tightened his hold on his mother, saw Jonas take another step forward and felt the rage building inside of him like before, the sound of June Bugs in his ears and if the man touched his ma-

The click of a shotgun being loaded startled the night and Cal looked to the darkness, saw the preacher lumbering forward.

"Henry," his ma whispered as she pushed him behind her.

"Now, Dess," he replied, stopping where he stood. "Don't get all sweet on me."

She opened her mouth, the strength the medicine had given her useless now.

"You do as my boy asked and hand over that bag," he paused, raised the shotgun. "Before I get testy."

Cal pulled away, stepped in front of her.

"You'd best go back the way you came," he said, his voice shaking, wishing Butler was here and wishing he would stay away. "Gran won't take kindly to this."

They laughed, and Jonas shook his head.

"Louise is probably passed out in that chair," he said. "And even if she was standing beside you, nothing would please her more than watching that Indian die."

Cal saw his mother jerk forward, saw her throw herself at Jonas Younts, her fists beating about his face and neck and shoulders, a cry coming from her that sounded almost like an animal, and it caught Henry Younts off guard, made him lower the shotgun before raising it again, the muzzle inches from her temple.

"Don't make me do it, Dess," he growled, and Cal stood frozen, terrified that any move would end his mother's life.

She stopped, turned slowly to look at him and Cal saw her raise herself up on her toes, saw her spit in his face.

"Dammit!" he cursed, swiping at his cheek, his frame so tight his arms began to shake with rage. "You're nothing but an ungrateful whore." Reaching out, he grabbed her elbow, pitched her towards the steps. "Get that bag if you want your boy to live past tonight."

Her face drained of color, she reached into the pocket of her dress.

"Ma-" he said weakly, thoughts of Butler haunting his mind.

"It's all right, Son," she said, and Henry Younts laughed.

"No, it ain't, boy."

Then his ma was taking the bag out, and Jonas was stepping forward, his hands greedy as he snatched it from her hand.

"Please," she said. "Don't hurt him-"

A moment passed in silence, the shotgun still gleaming in the moonlight as the preacher caught his breath, his eyes as sad as Cal had ever seen them.

"I ain't making no promises."

Cal felt his breath hitch, hopeful they wouldn't be able to find the shaman when Jonas smiled.

"I expect he'll be waiting under that cedar tree like you said."

His mother let out a sob, bent double now as she clutched her stomach.

"If you hurt him, I will hunt you down and I will kill you, Jonas Younts," she spat, her eyes on fire and he shook his head, tossed the medicine bag into the air and caught it again.

"Can't kill what's already dead."

Then they were backing up slowly, the shotgun still raised as Henry Younts took one last look at the woman he had loved before vanishing into the darkness again.

The sound of horses' hooves beating the earth made everything real again and Cal fell to his knees, great, wracking sobs that matched his heart making him senseless.

He sat that way, not knowing what to do when he felt his ma grab him under the arms, felt her lift him from the ground.

"Calvert," she whispered, her face streaked with tears. "You need to stop."

He shook his head, swiped at his face, thoughts of Jonas and Preacher hitting Butler, shooting Butler, killing Butler beating at his mind.

He remembered their walks through the woods, the branches like a roof above their heads. He remembered the moment they had found each of the totems, remembered the drum he had used when the eagle feather touched his ear and could not think straight.

I will hunt you down and I will kill you...

He knew his mother would keep her word, just as he knew he would be standing beside her when she put the gun to Jonas Younts' head.

And his father's.

"What are we gonna do?" he asked, shaking so badly his mother had to hug him. "We can't ever catch them now, can't ever warn him and-"

GO TO THE ISLAND IN THE MARSH

He felt his heart skid to a stop.

"Where?" he asked

BEYOND THE FALLS

"Why?" he asked, looking up at the trees, and then at his mother.

She grabbed his shoulders, her hope in his hands.

THEY'RE TAKING HIM THERE

CHAPTER
TWENTY-EIGHT

The autumn wind whipped my face as I held onto Dylan, my hands wrapped around his waist, the horse we had saddled racing through the night as the North Star hung overhead.

We had waited until we were sure Henry Younts and his son were gone before walking down the alley, the animals that remained after Orion had been set loose lifting their noses as we passed by.

"Have you ridden before?" Dylan asked.

I shrugged, slightly embarrassed. "Do the little ponies who do circles at the fair count?"

He cupped the back of his head, thinking about what to do.

"We'll go together, then," he said. "You just need to hold on tight."

Then he was opening the stall as he eased beside a large palomino, waiting until the animal got a sense of us before throwing a blanket across its back.

I watched in fascination as he led the horse into the alley and saddled it up, remembering that he had done this same thing before riding in a parade last spring and said a silent prayer of thankfulness.

Then he swung his legs over the horse's back, held his hand out as I stuck my foot in the stirrup and climbed up behind him.

"Don't let go."

I nodded, my arms tightening as he kicked the horse in the side and it stepped sideways, spun in a circle before galloping towards the barnyard and into the night.

I kept my head down, ducking beneath branches as the horse took off down the dusty lane we'd walked to Back Forty Farm on.

It wasn't long before Dylan reigned him in.

"Which way should we go?" he asked, turning the horse and I looked up at the stars, felt my brother with me for the first time since I'd come here.

"Go towards the river," I said. "We need to cross at the sandbar."

He looked at me over his shoulder, not asking if I was sure or why or even *how* before kicking the horse again.

Soon we were in an open field, speeding across the moon drenched hills and I felt the horse's fluid strides meld into a run, my braid flying out behind me as I wrapped my arms around Dylan's chest.

Then we were darting off into the woods, picking our way through the trees as the river rose to meet our ears and I was reminded of the time Henry Younts had stalked us from the opposite shore.

"There," he said, the lighter sand mixing with brackish water and the horse neighed, threw his head back as if to say he wanted no part of it.

Dylan made a clicking sound, urging him on and the horse took a step, jerking backwards as his hoof touched the water.

"I may have to lead him," he said, one hand closing over mine as he turned again and I nodded, slid off behind him.

Then I was stepping away, lifting my skirt as I began wading across the river, watching as the stars that had guided us began to dissolve into the lightening sky.

I heard the birds beginning to sing and looked back, saw the horse jerk away as Dylan tugged on his bridle.

One step closer and the water enclosed the animal's ankle. He pulled away again, reared up, his hind legs splashing us before he scrambled up the bank and back the way we had come.

"Damn," Dylan cursed, and I went to him, put a hand on his arm.

"It's okay," I said. "We're almost there now."

He looked at me, his eyes softening.

Moments later he was helping me up the other side and I was kicking off my wet shoes, the forest opening itself to me even as I tried not to think about what might be happening at this very moment on the island in the middle of the marsh.

I imagined Odessa wandering the dark, northern nights, imagined her looking for Butler and wished I had told him everything that was in my heart.

But he already knew.

"What are you thinking?" Dylan asked and I took his hand in mine.

"The same thing you are."

He stopped, turned to look at me.

"It'll be okay," he said. "He'll be okay."

I shook my head, my thoughts tangling on Cal and what he might have witnessed when Jamie and his father took the medicine bag.

"Hey," Dylan said, bending down so he could look in my eyes, "There was nothing we could do."

I covered his hand with my own, the strange power of the Whisper Stone looming before us.

"Now tell me what you're really thinking."

I looked down; pulled my lip between my teeth.

"It won't happen."

I met his gaze, my mind haunted.

"I won't let it," he said, his arms encircling me, his lips on mine as our kiss deepened, became desperate.

I felt him press against me and wrapped my arms around his neck, wishing we could become one person and I would never have to lose him again.

We stayed that way for what seemed like forever, our hearts beating against each other, the smell of his skin filling my senses until it created a world where we had always been, always would be and if I could carry it with me like the ring in my pocket-

"Sara!"

We pulled apart, looked around us for the person who had shouted as a figure moved between the trees.

"It's Andrew," I said, my heart speeding up. "If we follow him, we'll find the Whisper Stone."

He didn't ask questions, just followed me as I began to run and I prayed I could keep up my end of the bargain I'd made with her.

I caught sight of him ahead, thought about calling his name when we spilled into the snow-covered clearing, two figures standing in front of us.

Ethan Ebersole, his hand on his belt- and Andrew, a piece of Sara's nightgown in his hand as he touched the gun at his waistband.

They both spun when they saw us, Ethan's eyes going wide.

"What the hell?" he growled. "There's two of you now?"

Dylan didn't answer, just took a cautious step towards the men as Ethan unsheathed his knife.

"Take it easy," Dylan said, trying his best to defuse the situation just as he had at Huffs and a hundred other places and I felt my heart rise to my throat, where it seemed to choke me.

"What happened to Odessa?" I asked, my voice rising. "And Butler?"

He smirked, his arrogance still evident and I was reminded of all the times he'd hurt Amanda.

209

And Troy.

"Last I knew he was on the wrong side of Preacher Younts and his boy," he said.

I looked at Dylan.

"But I couldn't stay for the show... had to find Sara and ask her a few questions."

"Where is she?" Andrew said, his jaw clenched, his fingers flexing on the handle of his gun.

Ethan shook his head, "I was gonna ask you the same thing."

"Your brother and Esther were murdered last night."

Ethan chuckled under his breath, shook his head even as he adjusted his grip on the knife.

"Hadn't heard the news," he said. "But maybe Sara finally got sick of that whore and decided to do something about it."

Andrew drew his gun, his hand shaking with rage as Ethan lashed out with his knife.

"Stop!" I screamed, my thoughts flashing to Sara Bennett, and pushed myself between them.

I heard Dylan shout my name, felt his hand on my arm as he jerked me away, Ethan's knife flashing in the sun as it sliced across his stomach.

For a moment time stopped, and I saw Dylan look at me, blood oozing between his fingers as he tried to cover the wound and could not believe what had happened.

"No!" I screamed as he went to his knees, the sound coming from somewhere deeper than my physical body.

The next instant I heard Andrew's gun go off, watched as Ethan scrambled away into the woods, a bullet lodged in the tree just above his head.

My ears went numb, the sounds of the forest hushed around me and knew it had nothing to do with the medicine as I sank to the ground.

"He's hurt," Andrew said as he knelt beside me, his eyes wild as he wrestled with what to do.

I lifted a shaking hand, pushed my hair behind my ear and looked down at Dylan.

He'd rolled over onto his side, both hands covering his stomach and I reached out, turned him towards me.

"J," he rasped, and I put my hands over him, tried to stop the blood that seemed to be spreading everywhere.

"Rip off the bottom of your dress," Andrew instructed, and I looked at him, panic making my vision blurry. "We'll wrap him up best we can."

I nodded, my hands shaking as I tried to grab the green gingham and he took hold of my hem, ripped the fabric apart himself.

Moments later Andrew was propping him up as we unbuttoned his shirt. Then he was wrapping the gingham around his waist, and I found my mind flying to what might happen if we didn't find help soon.

"You're going to be okay," I said, my hands on his face now, staining his cheeks.

"That was a stupid thing you did," he whispered, trying to smile.

I laughed, my head a jumbled mess. "It's common knowledge I can be kind of a meathead."

"You're gonna give me a heart attack, you know that? Dead at twenty-five because of some barmaid I only met a year ago."

"Stop," I whispered, thoughts of our yellow bungalow and the rooster clock we'd hung above the sink sharpening my grief. "I promised Sara," I paused, pressed my lips to his forehead. "I promised her I'd save him."

I saw Andrew stir.

"What?"

I looked at him, wanting him to know everything.

"She's not here," I just managed.

"You know where she is?" Andrew demanded, rising on his knees now.

"It's not where she is," I said. "It's *when*."

"What do you mean?" he asked, desperate now.

"She'll be back," I said, my words almost nothing. "After your daughter is born."

I saw Andrew shake his head; unsure he'd heard right. Moments later his hand rose to rub at his chin, a smile appearing that seemed out of place with the scene around us.

"Our daughter..." he said.

"Wait for her," I said, my hands on Dylan's stomach again, pressing down as the blood soaked through the gingham.

Andrew nodded, his gaze lingering on my red hands, and I knew he was wondering how long it would take Dylan to die. "I'll get help."

I nodded again, my heart numb as he rose to his feet and disappeared into the woods.

I sat for several minutes, not knowing if time had slipped into minutes or hours or days, Dylan's head in my lap, watching his chest rise and fall, praying it wouldn't stop.

I put my face close to his, my lips against his temple.

"Don't let go," I whispered, and he opened his eyes.

"I said that once, didn't I?"

I nodded, my hand on his face as tears spilled over my cheeks and onto his, watching as the sun began to stretch between the trees.

A saw a red bird perch in a tree overhead and listened to its song, counting the moments since Andrew had left, watching Dylan's chest rise and fall again, more slowly this time, the front of my dress wet with his blood.

"J," I heard him moan and I moved, shifted on the moss to make him more comfortable, my hand stroking his hair and thought about the first time I'd seen him as he looked through Holly's window on the darkened roadway.

I saw him beside me as I woke up in the morning, the gray light just brushing his face, saw him before the fire in the Rook Cabin and felt a sob break free from my throat.

ADAM! HELP US!

I closed my eyes, listened for the voice that had told me to look up in Orion's stall, knowing if Andrew Karsten had left his gun, I wouldn't have hesitated to use it on myself.

"You must not think such things, Ogichidaa."

My eyes flew open, the words like ice on scalded skin.

At first there was nothing but silence, the dusky forest hesitant now.

And then he stood in front of me, tall and straight and strong, his long hair falling over his shoulders.

"How are you here?" I asked, unsure if he was real or if I'd fallen into a dream.

He smiled, "Cal told us where you were."

I blinked, saw that his clothing was torn and that blood had dried on his bottom lip.

"Butler-" I began, wondering if what I believed was possible.

"He is badly hurt," he said, and I tried to sit up but felt his hand on my shoulder, easing me into an upright position.

I swallowed, my hand resting on Dylan's chest as it continued to move shallowly beneath my fingertips.

"I don't understand," I asked again. "I thought Henry and his son hurt you. I thought you were...*gone*."

He shook his head, kneeling beside me now. "I asked you once what you were looking for."

I nodded. "I remember."

"I could not answer that question myself because I did not know," he said, looking over his shoulder as Odessa and Cal emerged from the sunlight. "But now I do."

"Dess," I cried, my heart racing as they ran to my side.

"Justine," Odessa whispered, her eyes sweeping to Dylan. "What happened?"

"Ethan Ebersole tried to kill Andrew," I managed. "He had a knife and I tried to get between them and..."

I saw her cover her mouth, saw her dark eyes widen as Cal went to his knees beside me.

"Nibwaaka," the boy said, turning towards the shaman. "You have to save him."

I saw Butler place a hand on his shoulder.

"No, Oshkinawe," he said. "*You* must save him."

I watched the boy shake his head. "But I don't know how."

"You do know," Butler said. "You just have to remember."

I looked into his eyes, my hand barely rising on Dylan's chest now as Cal jumped to his feet and ran off into the woods.

I saw my grandmother rise, saw her glance back at me before following her son.

"Do you want to know what happened on the island at the Falls?" Butler asked once we were alone, and I nodded, no longer afraid.

"I went there because Jonas Younts wanted something I could not give him, and now you and your brother must pay the price for it."

"But Odessa spent the rest of her life looking for you."

"No, Ogichidaa," he said, his eyes thoughtful. "I decided to take a different path."

I felt my mouth go dry, praying Dylan and I would get the same chance.

"Do not be worried."

I put a hand to my face.

"Dylan,"

"I will try and save him."

"And Henry Younts?"

He looked to the trees, the sound of footsteps heavy now as Odessa and Cal came running, yellow flowers in their hands.

"Will you do the same?"

I looked at him, wondering what he meant as the three people began to move around me.

"Quickly," the shaman instructed while taking the flowers they had gathered. "We must dress his wounds with these."

The next moment they were pulling the bloody strips of gingham from Dylan's skin, and I saw him start, heard him moan.

"Lie still," I whispered. "They're helping you."

He groaned, flinched as the leaves were placed against the open cut, Butler's voice rising as he began speaking in a language I didn't understand.

"His spirit is caught between this world and the next," Odessa said, her voice low as the shaman placed his hands on Dylan's shoulders. "He's calling it back."

I looked at her and she took my hand, squeezed it tightly as time began to flow backwards again, the feeling that I was swimming underwater making me sleepy.

"But I don't understand," I said, exhausted now as Butler's words seemed to float just out of reach. "When you said you couldn't answer me... what are you looking for?"

I felt Cal and Odessa lower me to the ground, felt bands of fatigue squeeze my body into something I was forced to surrender to.

"Them," he said, and I saw the three of them stealing away into the forest, making their long journey to the shores of the lake he had loved as a boy.

I smiled, my breathing measured as time turned to something that no longer made sense, warmth passing around my body in a muffled hush.

I was still for a long time before I felt Dylan move, and I turned my face to his, unsure if we were alone or if the others remained beside us.

"J?" I heard him say and felt the heaviness lift, felt the light pour around me as I opened my eyes.

Dylan was staring back at me, his gaze filled with wonder, and

I looked to his wound, saw that the skin had closed, the bleeding stopped.

I put my hands to my mouth, unable to make a sound as he pulled me against his chest.

"What happened?"

I held him, unable to tell him how much time had passed or if Andrew would ever come back or if we'd been dreaming the whole time.

"Butler healed you," I said, sitting up slowly. "And Cal and Odessa."

He seemed confused. "They did?"

I nodded, got unsteadily to my feet and watched him rise from the moss beside me like a man from his grave.

He shook his head, touched his stomach where his shirt hung in bloody strips.

"But I thought,"

"We were wrong."

We stood for a moment, watching the woods for the people we had come to love, knowing we would never see them again.

"We need to go," Dylan said, and I knew that he was right even as my heart longed for more.

Then we were standing on the stone, the trees whispering words Butler has spoken over us as Cal's small hands clasped a jar of cherry bark tea, his mother watching in amusement as I slipped into a pair of shoes that had fit before her son was born.

I saw Johnny following his sister out the door as his mother stood fuming, saw Abigail Karsten's bright eyes as she talked with Louise in the orchard, Sara's white nightgown flowing behind her as she abandoned the man she loved for the child she had yet to know.

I thought these things as the branches took hold of the breeze-their words giving life to the love that would lead us home.

I closed my eyes, fearing nothing now that the path had been made, and felt the great wind carry us away.

CHAPTER
TWENTY-NINE

I was standing on the Whisper Stone, watching as the silver veil unfolded around me, knowing it had brought us back to the moment just before the buckshot had splayed across my hip. I saw Henry Younts shift his shotgun and dropped to my belly, rolling to the side as buckshot peppered the snowy moss.

I heard Dylan shout my name and it caught Henry Younts' attention. Looking down, I thought I saw him smile as he raised the butt end of his shotgun over his head.

GO!

I saw my brother break loose from his mother, saw him rush towards Dylan and jumped to my feet.

"I have something!" I screamed, reaching into the pocket of the bloody dress I still wore.

"Something from Becky!"

At once he froze, his body going loose as though the wind had been knocked from him.

"Dess?" he just managed, his voice a whisper and I watched Troy stand up from behind, watched him swipe at his bloody lip as his eyes locked with mine.

"We found this in Orion's stall," I continued, holding the ring out in front of me.

Henry Younts narrowed his eyes, tightened his grip on the shotgun.

"She was riding Hector that day."

"No," I said, and he tightened his hold on the shotgun again, his eyes as black as I'd ever seen them.

"He threw her in that field at the bottom of the hill, just before you get to the bend in the river."

"That's not what happened," I said, taking another step forward and I saw his black eyes narrow, watched as my brother moved towards Pam, who pulled him against her chest as she backed away.

"She quarreled with me," Henry Younts grunted, his fingers flexing on the gun. "She wanted to ride Orion and I said he wasn't fit for it."

"She switched horses," I said, my eyes moving to Dylan as he rose slowly from the stone.

"She was riding Hector," he shook his head, confused to see me in the dress Odessa used to wear, talking about people who had been dead for over a century. "Abraham told me as much right before I shot the beast myself."

"He lied to you," Dylan said, beside me now. "He couldn't afford to lose his best horse."

I watched as Henry Younts loosened his grip on the shotgun, saw the front of it dip towards the ground and took my chance. "Her ring didn't fit under her new riding gloves-"

He made a sound in his throat, nodded. "I bought those for her birthday... cost as much as a horse itself-"

I put my hands up, took a step closer to him. "She was standing on the stool when Orion kicked it out from under her."

He shook his head, raised his shotgun again and I froze, the ring heavy in my hand.

"I found this on that little shelf in the corner, under the stars."

"The stars?" he repeated, his grip loose again.

"They were above the window," I said, hoping he would remember.

He shook his head, a slight laugh this time. "My boy helped Esther paint 'em when she got the fool notion in her head."

I glanced at Dylan, saw him nod almost imperceptibly.

"Here," I said, holding the ring out and he reached for it, his large hand cupping the tiny thing and I imagined it looked something like the love he'd felt for his wife.

I saw him turn the ring over, searching for something and when he found it, he laid the shotgun down slowly.

"There was a mark here in the gold," he said. "I didn't know until I'd given it to her, but she wasn't mad. She said it was just like life."

I swallowed, my heart in my throat.

"It wasn't your fault."

Henry Younts looked at me, his eyes lightening.

"My boy said as much."

I nodded, thinking of the man who had loved Esther Ebersole.

"I suppose I should have believed him."

I took a shaky breath, feeling like everything in my life had been leading up to this moment.

"You should go to him," I said. "To her."

He stood staring at me, his mind bending around what I'd just said.

"There's no place for me there," he whispered, his head still bent over the ring as he cradled it in his hands. "Not after what I've done."

I stood, thoughts of that long ago day at the community pool floating through my mind. And the little girl who clung to me, her eyes swollen from tears as she asked me where her father was.

"I forgive you," I said, felt her small hand slide into mine. "*She* forgives you."

He glanced up, seeming to understand and I looked to the

others, to the strange assembly of people who had helped me on my journey and found them frozen in place.

"That so?"

I nodded, watched as he slid the ring into the pocket of his shirt. Then he was stepping off the Whisper Stone, moving away from the snow covered clearing and I knew he was making his peace, knew he was going to a place from which he would never return.

I closed my eyes, felt a heaviness that had been inside of me for so long lift, a million dreams rising to take its place.

"Baby," I heard Dylan say as I went down on my knees, tears spilling over my cheeks as my brother ran to me, his face buried against my chest.

IT'S OVER

He looked up at me, his eyes watery as Dylan knelt beside us.

PROMISE?

He nodded, and I pulled him closer, kissed the top of his head.

We sat like that, the three of us locked together until I felt a hand on my shoulder.

I looked up, saw Troy behind me as his eyes sought Dylan's.

"Good job, Locke."

I saw Dylan smile, felt a laugh bubble up in my throat as another, softer voice caught our attention.

Sara Bennett, different than the last time I'd seen her, stood watching us from the edge of the clearing, her eyes bright.

"Do I get my happy ending now?"

"Mom," Amanda whispered, taking a step towards her and I could see she was confused, that she didn't understand what had changed.

"I kept my end of the bargain," Sara said, her eyes on me. "I hope you did the same."

I rose to my feet, nodded.

I saw Amanda stir, saw her look at her mother.

"What's going on?" she asked, and Sara smiled, took her daughter by the shoulders.

"Being your mother has been the greatest joy of my life," she said. "But your father is waiting."

"Waiting,"

"I wanted to give you the chance to live your life," she turned, her eyes on Troy. "With the man you love beside you."

I saw him move forward.

"You came back... on *purpose?*"

"I did," she nodded, reaching out to draw them both to her. "And I'd do it again."

I saw Amanda put her head on her mother's shoulder, tears on her cheeks.

"How do I do... *this* without you?"

Sara smiled; her eyes soft. "You don't."

I saw Amanda glance at Troy, confusion in her eyes.

"If you want me, you know where you can find me."

And then she was stepping on the Whisper Stone, and I saw her and Andrew walking by the creek that cupped the hill, the house shining like a crown on top of it.

"J," Dylan said, and I took his hand, looked up into his eyes and knew it was time to go.

"One more thing," I said, and Sara turned, her eyes questioning.

"Make sure they name the damn town Lantern Creek."

I heard her laugh; knew she would follow the path I'd made and felt someone beside me.

LET'S GET OUTTA HERE

I pulled my brother to my side, our thoughts tangling as we walked towards the truck. Once there, I stood with my hands splayed against the metal, unable to believe this simple object would carry me back to Friday night Euchre games, lemonade with Iris and Mallard's wide, bright smile.

I lifted my face to the sun, the little girl I'd come to find set free.

I took a breath, felt the wind gathering, and when I turned back to look at the Whisper Stone, Troy and Amanda were standing alone.

CHAPTER
THIRTY

"I don't know why you needed to borrow the laptop today," Holly said as she pushed open the door with a quick jab of her hip. "Didn't Dylan just buy you one?"

I shrugged; gave her the goofy smile I knew would throw her off.

"He's using it for class tonight, and I wanted to come out and see how things are going and maybe help with canoeing or something."

She looked at me, one eyebrow raised.

"You've promised such things before."

I gave the silly smile again, adjusted the purse that hung over my shoulder and my grip on the iced caramel latte I'd gotten at McDonalds.

"This time it's totally for real. Cross my heart and hope to die. Stick a needle,"

"No need to get graphic," she cut me off as we entered the dining hall where campers were enjoying their new and improved helpings of scrambled egg whites, turkey sausage and gluten-free pancakes.

I smiled, followed her through the cafeteria and into the counselor's lounge I'd frequented last summer when I wanted to find out why my life had suddenly gone to hell.

I didn't know why I'd wanted to come to Camp Menominee again and sit in the same chair beneath the same*Birds of Northern Michigan* clock, searching for something I wasn't sure existed.

Dylan and I had been lying low for the last few days. We'd done laundry, gone grocery shopping, and sat down to eat our grilled cheese and tomato soup dinner in a routine that felt odd in its simplicity. He'd gotten up for work, picked up where he'd left off in class while I did the same, my thoughts lingering on what we could tell and to whom.

And while a complete confession was sure to come, I wanted to enjoy this idyllic phase with Holly for as long as possible.

"Okay," she said while gesturing to the table with an exaggerated sweep of her arm. "You've got an hour and then I'm forcing one of those stinky orange vests over your head, shoving a sub-par paddle in your hand and pushing you towards the middle of the lake with a kid who hasn't seen water since the womb."

I scrunched up my face, "Who said dreams don't come true?"

She flashed me a thumbs up, then disappeared down the hallway and I turned, thinking back on what had happened, knowing I could never reclaim my life in the present until I returned to the past.

So, I sat down, opened the laptop while a chickadee sang me into the afternoon. More than once, I caught myself staring out the window, watching the girls in their swimsuits and one in particular who stood apart from the rest, an awkward rounding to her shoulders as she hugged her chest and remembered who I had once been.

The girl without a father.

Who'd found him at last.

It wasn't long before I discovered the website I'd stumbled across the summer before, wondering if my journey had changed anything, a skittish lilt to my heart when I thought about what I might find.

Scrolling down, I found the male nerd in his prime exactly as I'd left him- the blood red website banner screaming an altered title... *'Did Jonas Younts Get Away with Murder?'*

I skipped past the photos of the people and places I knew so well, the letters I'd discovered the summer before at the bottom of the site.

Dess,

I don't know if you will see this letter, but I was sitting at the tavern the other night when a strange man walked in who said he'd come from the north country way up by Superior way. He told me the strangest story about a lady living with a boy and an Indian an' I thought maybe it was you. When I told him my thoughts, he said I should write a letter and that he would take it to you the next time he checked his traps.

Much has changed since the night you ran away, and I want to say I don't hold nothin' against you for doing it. It was a hard life with Ma and me, and you must know that she went to her eternal reward the very evening you left us.

I found her in the chair the next morning, and when I looked at the bottle in her lap, she had drunk it bone dry. By the time Doc got there it was too late, and my only hope is that she is at peace again and with Pa.

That pretty gal what lived at the Ebersole farm was found shot alongside her husband and folks got it into their mind that Jonas Younts had done it. I don't think that young man could hurt a fly, but Sara Bennett saved his life by sayin' she saw Ethan Ebersole do the deed from her upstairs window.

Now, folks was quite troubled at first but it seems Ethan had cause to steal his brother's gold and when the Sheriff went looking for him, he had lit out and will likely not be found.

The shock of this seems to have changed Sara as she looked different the last time I saw her.It was not enough to keep the Karsten boy from marryin' her, and the two have taken a house together not far from the big farm where they seem mighty content.

I must say the home place has suffered since you and the boy have gone, but of late I've met a gal who seems taken with me and we are working hard at turning it around.

I write this letter not knowing if you will ever see it but tell the boy I miss him and that I hope you are happy.

Your brother,

Johnson

I sat back against the chair, hardly aware of my surroundings before reading the second.

Johnny,

I did get your letter and was very pleased to have news of my home place.

It was a shock to hear of Ma, but I knew that bottle would be the end of her, as were the many sorrows she carried inside of her heart. Like you, I hope she has found peace at last.

We have been living for the past year in a cabin built on the shores of the Gichigami. It is the land of the shaman's people and even though his name is no longer spoken, we have been visited twice by those who know him and are curious about us.

I write to tell you that you have a niece, born in high summer and under the Berry Moon. She is lovely and strong, and Cal watches over her with a fierce protection that makes me proud. My only wish is that she will grow into a woman who will be welcome at your table should she ever find herself in the land I still see in my dreams.

We are content, Brother, as you seem to be, and I hope to one day see the wild woods and hills of the home place again. I pray for Sara and Andrew's happiness, and for Jonas and his father, who are never far from my thoughts.

Much Love,

Dess

I sat looking at the screen as the clock ticked away behind me, thinking of Butler and Odessa and Cal and the little girl they had welcomed on the shores of the Gichigami. I thought about Louise and Johnny and Sara and Andrew, their faces lost to time and slung my purse over my shoulder, sure Holly would give me crap for ditching canoe duty again.

Five minutes later I was walking towards the Heap- unearthed from its unholy resting place because it was my only viable option.

Still mildly surprised when she sprang to life, I said a small prayer that she would remain so before pulling out of the parking lot and heading south on 23.

Twenty minutes later I pulled up outside of Pam's house.

"Justine," she said after opening the door, a smile on her face that said I would always be welcome here as Rocky squirmed his way around her legs.

"Can my brother come out and play?" I asked while leaning down to scratch behind his ears.

She crossed her arms. "Aren't you a little old for that?"

I laughed. "I promise to return him in the same condition he left in."

One glance at the Heap and she shook her head.

"Don't make promises you can't keep."

The next second Adam was pushing past us and rushing towards the Heap, Rocky on his tail, a grin on his face that said he was excited to climb inside and see if anything exploded when we tried to drive away.

WHERE ARE WE GOING?

I threw an arm around his shoulder, ruffled the top of his hair like I always did.

"You'll see."

We continued south along the shores of Lake Huron, the blues and grays and silvers of the water mixing until it became the color of Dylan's eyes and I thought back to the time we'd spent with Odessa, trying to remember where the remains of the Cook house might be.

A dirt road that hugged the hills caught my attention.

THAT WAY

I glanced at him sharply, saw he had his arm hanging out the window as Rocky stuck his head between us from the back seat.

"How do you know?"

JUST A FEELING

I shook my head as I turned down the road, sure we were crazy when I saw a misshapen tree I remembered from my painful walk to the Jennison Barn on market day.

Next came a field with a large cottonwood beside it, a wooded hillside stretching towards the remains of the Rook Cabin.

The dirt road ended, and I stopped, stepped out and looked back the way we had come.

I remembered the soft glow of the windows as I stood in the yard, Johnny's gun in my hand as the wolf watched us from the shadows. I saw the cool breeze that blew Esther's dark hair as we walked in the afternoon light, a handkerchief hidden within the cuff of her sleeve.

I saw all of this and knew where I was, knew that this place had always been here, hidden until I was ready to see it.

I took my brother by the hand, opened the back door for Rocky and led them into the trees, remembering the day we had buried our necklaces in the yellow wood.

It wasn't long until we saw the house and I paused, undone by how it had changed, knowing deeper that everything remained the same.

IT'S INSIDE

I turned to my brother.

"What is?"

He shook his head.

I'M NOT SURE

I took a breath and made my way towards the house. Placing one palm against the door, I pushed it open and saw Louise on the other side, her face red as she bustled from room to room. Another step and Odessa came forward, her long braid over her shoulder as she called me to breakfast.

"Hello?" I said, the single word echoing in the empty space, and I waited, expecting to hear Cal's voice in response.

I turned, motioned for Adam to enter and he did, his eyes taking everything in as Rocky pushed his way around us.

IT FEELS LIKE-

"Home," I said, reaching back and taking his hand, leading him from room to room before finally entering the bedroom I'd slept in over a hundred years before. Once there, I took a deep breath, a million memories flooding back as I put a hand to my face.

SIS?

"It's okay."

WHAT HAPPENED HERE?

I looked at him.

"Everything."

He stared at me, his large eyes reminding of Cal and the night he had given me the snakeskin. I remembered him telling me about a floorboard in the corner, remembered that he said he kept the snakeskin safe there.

I went to where I remembered it to be and fell to my knees. Prying the board up with my fingers, it came loose, a cloud of dust kissing my nose.

Moments later I was flat on my stomach, reaching into the darkness.

BE CAREFUL

I looked down, my fingers fluttering for purpose until they brushed against something cold and square and hard.

WHAT IS IT?

I shook my head, reached lower, my hand closing around a metal box.

I sat up quickly, laid the thing between us on the plank floor and opened it as Rocky came to sit beside us.

THERE'S A LETTER

I looked inside, saw the piece of paper folded into quarters and remembered mom handing me the same thing over the backseat of our brown Pontiac, the smell of chlorine suffocating me.

OPEN IT

I took it out with shaking hands and looked at Adam.

IT'S OKAY

I nodded, swallowed quickly, and unfolded it.

Justine,

I gasped, unable to believe the letter was meant for me even as I began to read it aloud.

It's been a long time since I last saw you, but I want you to know that I've thought of you every day since.

The shaman told me why you came to us- and I must say a piece of my heart always knew you were much more than a friend.

I've grown up now and have a family of my own. You wouldn't recognize me as the boy who was always underfoot, but something told me to bring my sister to the home place and here we are, writing a letter to a person who won't read it until long after we've gone to the place Ma and Butler went before us.

I know that one day you will come here with your brother, and I know you will find the letter and read it with a heart that is ready to hear all that I wasn't able to tell you in the short time we spent together.

I want you to know that my mother and Butler- the man I came to call my father- lived a long and happy life together. Even though our family was not like others, we came to be accepted by the clan of our ancestors and lived safely among them for many years.

My father often talked about you, and before he died, he gave me three shells that were sacred to his people.

If you look inside the box, you will find two of them.

My sister carries the third.

These are his gifts for the Children of the Falling Leaves Moon, so that when they walk between the worlds, they will never be alone.

Always,

Cal

I sat for a long while before I looked inside the box, Adam beside me, his mind silent.

I closed my eyes, thought about that morning when Dylan had left for work. He'd held me close before kissing me deeply at the door, our time in the past strengthening our faith in the future.

Then I was taking out the shells and turning them over in my hand, feeling the distant sea they had come from as surely as the man who had carried them.

ARE YOU READY?

I shook my head, not wanting to leave as Rocky pushed his head under my hand.

THEY'LL ALWAYS BE WITH US

I took a breath, his words releasing something inside of me that wanted to hold on forever.

"Like Dad?" I asked and he smiled, his eyes soft in the rising light.

YES

Then I was getting slowly to my feet, a thousand memories taking flight and settling in the sky, where they would shine like the stars Esther had made a home for so long ago.

We were halfway to the Heap when my cell phone rang and I stopped, dug it out of my back pocket, a smile painting my lips when I saw who it was.

"Hey," Dylan said, obviously relieved that I had answered. "Where are you?"

I glanced at the sky, thinking he might have come home for his lunch, loving that he still worried about me even though the most exciting thing I'd done in the past three days was travel back in time to make peace with a tortured soul who had hunted my family for generations.

"You'd never believe it."

A pause. "Did you find what you're looking for?"

My heart warmed.

He got it.

Got me.

Like always.

"I'll be here when you get home."

Which made me want to get there all the faster.

EPILOGUE

Dylan and I were married beneath the maple trees in our backyard on an afternoon in September, their leaves touched with a brilliance that seemed ready to bloom.

I wore a simple dress that fell past my knees, a bouquet of forget-me- nots in my hand to honor the couple who had married on the winter solstice so many years ago.

My hair hung in a loose braid Odessa might have plaited for me, while a lone guitar player stood at the edge of the tent Mallard had put up the day before.

I glanced over at the roughneck in question, my arm clasped in his as I waited for the music to start.

"You sure you wanna go through with this?" he asked, his hair and mustache slicked down, his requisite white muscle shirt replaced with a worn denim button down. "It's not too late to back out."

I smiled, drawing him close to my side.

"Now that you mention it, that guy standing at the end of the aisle looks like he's up to something."

I heard my brother laugh.

"I know this is gettin' official real fast," Mallard said while stroking his mustache. "But I don't trust him any farther than I can fucking throw him."

I looked at him sharply. "Little ears!"

GIVE ME A BREAK

ADAM-

I HEAR WORSE STUFF AT SCHOOL

I bit my lip, tried to suppress a smile even as I scanned the small crowd for the man whose hair caught fire with the sun.

And then the music began, a simple song about finding love right where we were and I took a step, my knees shaking, and felt Mallard tighten his grip.

"You've got this, Flats."

Another step and Adam's hand tightened in mine. And then Dylan was before me, his eyes locked on me, and it stopped me in my tracks.

He was so beautiful, his face marked with a love that can only come with loss and I thought about the man that he was- tender and steady and strong and stubborn and knew his shortcomings were no greater than my own.

Then I was standing in front of him, Dave and Holly on either side while Iris took center stage and extended her hands, inviting everyone to sit down.

I hadn't known my grandmother could help us in this matter, but it seemed at some point in the recent past she had added 'Ordained Minister' to her extensive list of accomplishments.

I heard her speaking words, heard her ask who gave me in marriage as my mother stood, her face strong and still.

"Her father and I."

I bowed my head, overcome by his presence as it filled the air around me.

I saw the young boy who had found me in the field, his mother dancing in her best pink dress and the man who loved them both, his dark eyes holding all the pieces of my broken heart.

I stood, my hand in Dylan's as he promised to love, honor, and cherish me- things he had already done a thousand times over.

And then there were rings, the simple bands reminding me of the love that had set my family free.

I watched as Dylan slid it over my knuckle, his touch promising that everything would be different when we laid beside each other tonight.

And then he leaned forward, his hands cupping my face as he kissed me like he had in front of the fire at the Rook Cabin.

Moments passed and we broke apart, watching the faces of our friends as they clapped for us, walking back the way we had come, only this time together.

We stood beneath the maples in our backyard as people drifted to the tables Holly had helped me decorate, the food Pam had spent days preparing piled high on their plates.

I stopped, lingering near Dylan's family as his sister stood up to hug me.

"I'm so happy," she said, her arms almost crushing me, and I wondered what her mother was thinking, knowing it would take time to understand all the things Dylan had told her.

And that was okay, because she was here, looking splendid in a dress that cost more than mine, Michael Locke beside her, the blue eyes he shared with his son crinkling when he saw me.

And then we were moving again to Pam and Mallard and Adam and Mom, and I wondered at the strange circumstances that had brought these people together before a hand clasped down on my elbow.

"Holy friggin crud, Squirt," Holly hissed, pointing to a man who stood on the edge of the lawn. "He must have heard there was a party. Of course, he did. He's a *party kind of guy...*"

"Party?" I asked. "This isn't just a random *party,*"

She waved a hand at me. "Sure, it is... just go with it."

I frowned. "Dylan invited him. He plays guitar and we thought he could give the other guy a break and,"

"Who cares what you thought. He can't see me and he sure as hell can't give the other guy a break."

"Holly," I said, the truth slowly dawning on me. "Please tell me you didn't date both of them."

"Well..."

"Was this before or after Joe from Cheboygan?"

She dug one toe into the ground, resplendent in her cherry red 'bridesmaid' dress. "I might have broken up with one for the other but there's *no way* they could know that. *No way* unless Jen Reddy happened to say something when she ran into them at the Deer Hunt Lounge."

I stood, staring at her while people continued to mingle around us.

"Don't judge."

I laughed, put my forehead against hers. "Never a dull moment."

"You should talk."

I smiled. She had me there.

"I'll just make like a wallflower and stay on this side of the tent."

"I don't think 'blending in' was the plan when you bought that dress."

She winked at me, giggled before slinking off to find Dave and I scanned the crowd again, searching for the man who had swum with me to the middle of Tamarack Lake.

"I heard someone got hitched."

The voice jolted me, sent me spinning where I saw Troy standing over my shoulder, Amanda at his side.

"You're here!" I cried, and he came to me, pulled me into a hug.

"Sorry we're late," Amanda apologized. "Traffic was backed up on the Bridge."

"And I had to clear some trees for our new place," Troy offered, his eyes holding mine for a beat as we stood in the snow covered clearing on Mackinac Island.

Then Dylan was there, shaking Troy's hand and I watched the two of them together, thinking how extraordinary our lives were as we made plans to visit on our budget-friendly honeymoon to Pictured Rocks.

"Aren't you going to introduce me?" Holly asked, no longer concerned with blending in and I knew she must have spotted Troy from a mile away.

I watched her take his hand in greeting as Dave strolled over, sweetly oblivious as he caught my husband's attention with talk of the new guy at their Thursday night basketball game who couldn't make his layups.

I stood watching everything unfold around me, feeling as though the day was perfect aside from the one thing I couldn't fix, a heaviness settling on my chest as Mallard stood on a chair and invited everyone back to Huffs for a nightcap.

I watched Iris saunter into view, saw her put her hand on Shaw's back and whisper something in his ear before coming to me, and in my mind, we were surrounded by the flowers in her garden as Joey did a figure eight swish around my legs.

"So, how does it feel?" she asked.

I smiled, pulled my long braid over my shoulder. "Like it's meant to be."

I felt her hand close over mine, felt her shoulder touch me. "You did good, Muffet."

I closed my eyes, imagining for a moment that her son was with us.

"Now you have everything you've ever wanted."

I felt her words sting my heart. "Not everything."

She squeezed my hand. "I know the feeling."

I looked up, saw her eyes searching for the same person.

"Maybe it's for the best," she said, and I felt my breath catch, stunned by her words.

"Iris,"

"He would've had a helluva time letting you go."

My nose began to tingle, and I reached up to touch it.

"You coming to Huffs," she asked, a twinkle in her eye. "No one would blame you if you wanted to hit the hay a little early."

I laughed, smoothing my dress as my mother appeared over her shoulder.

"We'll stop by later," I assured her, and she nodded, her gaze traveling between us before leaving us alone.

We stood side by side for a long while looking up at the sky when she finally spoke.

"Everything was beautiful."

I nodded.

"Dylan loves you," she said, a tone in her voice that said she was lost. "That's all I ever wanted."

"Mom,"

"I'm sorry about what happened with Paul and Meg."

"Don't-"

"I got so caught up in what I was feeling that I didn't think about anything else," she paused, looked down at her hands. "Including you."

I felt my breath catch in my throat.

"And I think that's what I regret the most."

I reached over, took her hand.

"Why am I still afraid?"

"It's okay,"

"I don't know how to stop *looking* for him."

I leaned back, felt the weight of the past settle in a space that made sense.

"Me, either."

I felt her squeeze my hand as Iris had done a moment before. "How do we let him go?"

I shook my head, Sara Bennett's words coming back to me.

"We don't." I said. "We need to remember. And we need to live."

A pause. "What if I don't know how to do that?"

I looked at the woman my father had loved, standing alone with me in the dark as we'd always been.

"We'll figure it out together."

She nodded; her fingers intertwined with my own as our hearts made a new path.

A light touch to her back and she turned, followed where the others had gone and I wandered to the edge of the yard, to the place where the warm glow from our windows spoke of the ordinary life that now belonged to me.

I took a deep breath, felt the air cool my skin.

I don't know how else to be...

I didn't either, but there were people who had gathered down at Huffs who would help with talks of mushroom hunting and Butterfly Weed and the latest level they'd gotten to on the Mountain Troll of Terror video game. There would be nights spent under the close and often unqualified supervision of a roughneck named Mallard Brauski and friends to visit while they carved out a life on banks of the Au Train River.

I stood, looking up at the stars and felt my husband beside me.

"J," he said, and I turned, found him staring up at the same thing I was. "They're waiting for us."

I nodded, opened my hand and looked down at the shell I'd been saving for the child of Sara Bennett.

And the third, tucked away in my nightstand until the time of the Budding Moon.

I watched as Dylan's hand sought my stomach, his fingers splayed as if to protect the small life that had been growing there since our night in the Rook Cabin, a gentle rounding of flesh that would remain our secret until this night of a thousand stars.

"Are you ready?" he asked, his eyes alive in the darkness.

I smiled, my lips seeking his.

"I always was."

THE END

239

ACKNOWLEDGMENTS

So many people have stepped forward to make this moment possible for me, and I'm grateful to each and every one of them. Thank you to Nola Nash for being my book BFF. I don't know how I would navigate this world without you. Thanks to Terry Shepherd for living up to his name by guiding me through the maze of hybrid publishing. Plus, you're a really cool Michigan guy! Appreciate you and your eternal optimism. Special thanks to Denise Birt for taking some of the author load off my shoulders by not only being a gifted graphic artist, but also a kind and supportive friend. Thanks also to my editor, Wendee Wendt, your keen eye for detail has been my salvation, and to Pam Stack for welcoming me into her fabulous Authors on the Air Global Network.

Thanks also to my author friends Wade Rouse, Kiersten Modglin, Shanessa Gluhm, Rob Samborn (collaboration is FUN) Alison Ragsdale, Suzy Garner, Sharon Bippus, Hayla Mostrum, Margy Eickoff, Patricia Sands, Grace Sammon, Sharon Gloger Friedman, Jill Hannah Anderson, Benny Sims, Seth Augenstein, Carla Vergot, Shannon Jump, Nancy Johnson and Renea Winchester for offering me a soft place to fall when I want to cry or rejoice or do anything in between. The world would be a lonely place without you guys in it!

Thanks also to my Kemp Camp Street Team Members and all the joy you give me. I'm so honored to be your Head Counselor and hope for many more years around the campfire!

Thanks to the library staff that have welcomed me, the book

clubs that have made a place for me at their table, the farmer's markets and festivals that have allowed me to participate and the countless readers who have reached out to say my stories made an impact in their life. You are the reason I do what I do.

Finally, I'd like to thank my family for putting up with the long hours spent in front of the computer doing 'something or other.' It take a village to put these books together, and you have been my strongest support throughout it all. Mom, Dad, Scott, Stone, Megan, Analiese and Aubrey... I love you!

Laura Kemp

May, 2022